"I could vote for Joe," Samantha told Damont.

Damont laughed. "For Joe? But he's not even running," Damont insisted.

"But he could," David insisted just as strongly.

"Yeah," Wishbone chimed in. "He could, all right. In fact, Joe would make a terrific class president."

Damont sighed and turned to Joe. "Tell this guy you're not running," he said, jerking a thumb at David.

Joe thought for a moment. Finally, he said, "I could run."

Damont looked at him. "You'd run against me?" Suddenly, he broke out into laughter. "That's the most ridiculous thing I ever heard."

"In fact," Joe said, "I think I'll sign myself up tomorrow at school. . . ."

Other books in the Adventures of **WISHBONE**™ series:

The Adventures of WISHBONE™

The Mutt in the Iron Muzzle

by Michael Jan Friedman
Inspired by *The Man in the Iron Mask*
by Alexandre Dumas

WISHBONE™ created by Rick Duffield

SCHOLASTIC INC.
New York Toronto London Auckland Sydney

Edited by Kevin Ryan

Copy edited by Jonathon Brodman

Cover design by Lyle Miller

Interior illustrations by Arvis Stewart

Cover concept by Kathryn Yingling

Wishbone photograph by Carol Kaelson

ISBN 0-590-63473-9

12 11 10 9 8 7 6 5 4 3 2 1   8 9/9 0 1 2 3/0

Printed in the U.S.A.   40

First Scholastic printing, September 1998

Cover illustration copyright © 1997 by Ferenc Suto
Cover and book design by Paul Zakris
The text for this book is set in 12-point Garamond Three

For Brett, who hates injustices

FROM THE BIG RED CHAIR . . .

Oh . . . hi! Wishbone here. You caught me right in the middle of some of my favorite things—books. Let me welcome you to THE ADVENTURES OF WISHBONE. In each of these books I have adventures with my friends in Oakdale and imagine myself as a character in one of the greatest stories of all time. This adventure takes place during the same time period as the first season of my television show, when Joe and his friends are twelve and in sixth grade. *THE MUTT IN THE IRON MUZZLE* is inspired by the classic tale *THE MAN IN THE IRON MASK*, written by Alexandre Dumas. In this story I imagine that I am Philippe, twin brother of the king of France. This is an exciting tale about courage, mistaken identity, and Philippe's rise from prisoner to king.

You're in for a real treat, so pull up a chair and a snack and enjoy reading!

Chapter One

As Wishbone dashed up a rise in the green terrain of Jackson Park, his heart started to beat faster and faster with excitement. After all, he knew what was on the other side of the rise.

When he got to the top, the little white terrier with brown spots bunched his muscles, leaped into the blue sky, then descended to the downhill side. There he feasted his eyes on one of the most beautiful sights in the world.

A baseball field!

There it was, sprawling lazily in the mellow September sunlight. It was defined by two white foul lines and a big, chainlink backstop. Its base paths and its pitcher's mound were covered with dark orange clay. The clay made the four bases and the pitcher's rubber look clean and white despite the beating they had taken all summer.

A baseball field!

Where kids had performed their deeds of glory since long before Wishbone had been a puppy. Where the power of a thousand bats had challenged the speed of a thousand balls, often with explosive results. Where bright mornings and golden afternoons melted into timeless twilights.

A baseball field!

Wishbone raised his nose and smelled the sweetness of the freshly cut grass. He sniffed at the rich, earthy scent of the dirt, and he savored the tang of the sun-warmed metal bleachers along both foul lines.

"You know," he said, "it just doesn't get much better than this."

Looking back over his shoulder, he saw Joe, Samantha, and David making their way over the rise. They were carrying the same bats and gloves and balls they had been playing with for the last few months. All three of them were grinning with anticipation.

Joe, Wishbone's best friend, was pretty easygoing and laid back most of the time. But on the baseball diamond, he really came alive. That was because he was a terrific athlete. Even with all his physical ability, though, he never forgot to be a team player.

David was the kind of kid who could build almost anything from the simplest supplies on hand. If someone had a difficult situation and needed a really neat invention to solve it, David was the guy to call on.

Samantha had an ability to relate to people that made her very special. Wishbone had never met anyone who didn't have a good word to say about Sam. For that matter, he had never met anyone who Sam didn't like.

All three friends had spent most of the day in school. With summer over, it was time to crack the books again. The cold days of winter were right around the corner. That made it even more of a thrill to come out to the park and knock the ball around.

"I'll bat first," David suggested, as they descended the rise and came to the level ground of the outfield.

"That's only fair," Joe agreed. "I got to bat first last time. And Sam hit first the time before."

Samantha elbowed David good-naturedly. "Just don't hit too many over Joe's head. He gets dizzy easily."

"Hey," said Joe, "you hit 'em as far as you want. Wishbone *likes* chasing those long fly balls."

"I do, indeed," said the terrier. "As a matter of fact, the longer the better."

What could be more fun than running after baseballs in the outfield? Some of the game's greatest players had made names for themselves by doing that. Of course, Wishbone was famous only in his own neighborhood—but that was more than he could say for *some* dogs.

Besides, it wasn't a hunger for fame that sent him leaping through the outfield. It was the joy of snatching the ball in his teeth. It was the thrill of racing back to the infield as fast as he could, legs churning while the kids cheered him on.

Now, that was living!

As the kids had agreed, David came to bat first. Samantha played midway between first and second base. Joe positioned himself between second and third. Wishbone planted himself in center field, where he sat with his tail wagging, eager for some action.

It wasn't long in coming. The first time David tossed the ball up and hit it, he sent a lazy fly out to left center. Joe leaped for the ball, but it was out of reach of his mitt. So Wishbone was called on to run it down and bring it back to the infield.

"All in a day's work," he said.

David hit a few more good shots to the outfield,

and Wishbone retrieved them all. He hit some grounders to Joe and Samantha, too. Then Samantha came up to home plate, and David took her place between first and second.

Samantha was a line-drive hitter, but the balls she hit still rolled a long way—at least, when there was no one in the outfield quick enough and tireless enough to run them down before they went very far. Fortunately, Wishbone was both quick enough *and* tireless enough.

Finally, it was Joe's turn to hit. As he stepped up to the plate, Samantha assumed his position between second and third and pounded her glove.

"Okay, Joe!" she shouted. "Let 'er rip!"

"Show 'em where you live, Joe!" David yelled.

"Yeah!" cheered Wishbone. "Put a jolt into it!"

Normally, Wishbone wouldn't have considered it very polite for Joe's friends to holler at him. But he had learned that on a baseball field, it was good manners to shout things at the batter. It showed that you were rooting for him or her to do well.

Of course, Wishbone thought with pride, *Joe always does well. He's the best baseball player in the sixth grade.*

And I don't say that just because I taught the boy everything he knows.

With his first swing, Joe rapped the ball right at David, who barely snatched it up as he ducked. With Joe's second swing, he sent the ball sailing high and far beyond second base.

Wishbone liked to think of himself as a pretty good outfielder. But even *he* took a long time catching up with the ball. When Wishbone finally brought it back, Joe was shading his eyes—and staring at something on the far side of the backstop.

"What is it?" Wishbone asked, wagging his tail with anticipation. "A rabbit? A cat?"

He sniffed the air, but he didn't smell either of those things. Then he got close enough to see that Joe was looking at one of the open stretches of grass. Following his pal's gaze, Wishbone saw that a few youngsters in pale blue uniforms had begun tossing a ball around.

The kids looked a bit older than Joe and his friends. They were seventh-graders, if Wishbone was any judge of such matters.

But why was Joe staring at them in that odd way? He had a Little League uniform of his own from last spring—a red-and-white one. Wishbone liked it better than what those other kids were wearing.

"Come on, Joe," he said. "I've got the ball, see? You still have a whole bunch of swings coming."

But Wishbone's best friend didn't answer. It seemed he couldn't stop staring at the kids in the blue uniforms. David and Sam noticed, too.

"What's going on?" asked David.

Samantha jerked a thumb in the direction of the older kids. "Don't you see who they are?" she asked.

David looked a while longer. Then he frowned, as he realized what Sam was talking about.

"The seventh-grade traveling team," David said.

"Ah," Wishbone said. "So that's who they are."

He'd heard the story almost as soon as Joe was big enough to put on a baseball mitt. Every autumn, the Oakdale Little League put together a team of the best players in the sixth and seventh grades. Then it sent that team all over the state to compete with the best players in other towns.

Back when Joe's father was a boy, he had been on the Oakdale traveling team. That squad had gone all the way to winning the state championship.

Of course, it was pretty tough to make the team as a sixth-grader, considering how many good seventh-graders were around. But Joe was the best player his age in Oakdale. If anyone could make it, he could.

Joe really wanted to play on that team. The terrier could tell by the look on the boy's face as he watched the older kids practice. In fact, Joe wanted that honor more than anything.

Just then, Wishbone smelled a familiar scent in the air. Turning upwind, he confirmed the bad news his nose had given him.

"Damont alert," he said.

Sure enough, Damont Jones came walking along a path through the trees. When he saw Joe and his friends, he smiled the smile that always made Wishbone's fur stand on end.

Damont couldn't be trusted under the best of circumstances. And when he smiled that big smile of his, the wisest thing to do was to turn around and run. Unfortunately, no one ever did.

Two other boys were walking behind Damont.

One was Colby, a big kid with a dark-haired crew cut. The other was Marcus, a tall, skinny boy with a shock of blond hair. Both Colby and Marcus had their arms wrapped around brown-paper shopping bags. The bags were full of something, though Wishbone couldn't smell what it was.

"Hey, guys," said Damont, as cheerful as Wishbone had ever seen him. "Whaddaya say? Is this a great day or what?"

Joe's eyes narrowed with suspicion. He had heard that kind of opening remark before. "You want something from us, don't you, Damont?"

Damont looked shocked. "Me? Want something from you? No way. In fact, I wanted to *give* you something."

"For how much?" asked Joe.

"Yeah," David chimed in. "How much is this little gift going to cost us?" He dug into his pockets and displayed what he had found there. "I've only got fifty cents."

Damont heaved a sigh. "You guys wound me, you know that? I wouldn't dream of taking your hard-earned money. No . . . what I'm about to give you is out of the goodness of my heart."

Wishbone cocked his head. "Oh, yeah? This I gotta see."

Damont motioned and Colby came forward. He reached inside his bag and handed a big, round button to Joe. Then he gave one to Samantha, and another one to David.

When Colby was done, it was Marcus's turn to dole out the goodies. Except, instead of buttons, he handed out bumper stickers. And then came pennants—the kind Joe hung on his bedroom walls.

David read his button. "'Put Jones on Your Team'?"

Sam grunted as she inspected a bumper sticker. "'Damont's the One'?"

Joe looked at Damont. "What's all this about?"

Damont rolled his eyes. "Don't you guys know anything? The sixth grade gets to elect a class president. And I intend to win the election by a landslide."

Joe held up his button, his pennant, and his bumper sticker. "But where did you get all this stuff?"

Damont blew on his nails and polished them against his shirt. "It wasn't all that hard, really. That is, if you've got an uncle in the printing business—which I do."

"Wait a minute," said Samantha. "That's not fair. How are the other candidates supposed to compete with all this . . . this junk?"

Damont shrugged. "Let them find their own uncles," he suggested.

Sam crossed her arms and frowned at him. "I'm serious. What chance do the other candidates have when you're giving out all this stuff?"

"First of all," Damont told her, "there's nothing wrong with getting your message out. Freedom of speech is what this country was built on. And second," he chuckled, "there *are* no other candidates."

"So far," said David.

"Okay," Damont conceded, "so far."

"And there's still a couple of days for other candidates to sign up," David went on.

"Whatever," said Damont. He held his hands out, palms up. "So? Can I count on your vote?"

"That depends," Samantha replied. "What's your platform?"

Damont looked at her as if she'd just grown another head. "Platform?" he echoed.

"What I mean," said Sam, "is where do you stand on the issues?"

Damont tilted his head. "Issues? What issues?"

Now it was Samantha's turn to roll her eyes. "If we don't know what you stand for, why should we vote for you?"

"Because you'll be a dork if you don't," Damont told her. "Everybody who's anybody is going to be voting for me. I mean, what else can you do—vote for *nobody?*"

Samantha didn't have a good answer for that. Then she turned to Joe, and her expression changed. "I could vote for *Joe*," she told Damont.

Damont laughed. "For Joe? But he's not even running."

"But he could," David pointed out.

"Yeah," Wishbone chimed in. "He could, all right. In fact, Joe would make a terrific class president."

"But he's not running," Damont insisted.

"But he could," David insisted just as strongly.

Damont sighed and turned to Joe. "Tell this guy you're not running," he said, jerking a thumb at David.

Joe thought for a moment. Finally, he said, "I *could* run. In fact, I *will* run."

Damont looked at him. "You'd run against *me?*" Suddenly, he broke out into laughter. "That's the most ridiculous thing I ever heard."

But Wishbone heard something in Damont's voice that wasn't amusement. Unless he was mistaken—and what were the odds of that?—Damont was scared stiff that Joe would run against him.

David poked a finger against Damont's chest. "I bet Joe would beat you," he declared. "Hands down."

"That'd be the day," Damont replied.

"And he'd be a better class president," David added. He turned to Joe. "Wouldn't you?"

"Maybe I would at that," Joe agreed. "In fact, I think I'll sign myself up tomorrow morning at school."

Damont scowled. "Look, I can see I'm wasting my time here. You guys vote for whoever you want. Me, I've got a campaign to run." With a wave to Colby and Marcus, he turned and headed toward another group of sixth-graders playing nearby.

Wishbone watched them leave. He was certain that Damont didn't want Joe running against him. The question was . . . what was Damont going to do about it? How was he going to keep Joe from competing with him?

"Hmm . . ." Wishbone said to himself, settling into the grass. "Two rivals going head to head for an important position—and a plan to keep one of them out of the running. Why does that scenario sound so familiar?"

Then it came to him. He had encountered the same situation in the novel *The Man in the Iron Mask*, written more than a hundred years ago by a French author named Alexandre Dumas.

The Man in the Iron Mask was about the wealthy lords and ladies living in the seventeenth century who schemed and plotted in the royal circle of the French king. It was about power and responsibility. And it was about an innocent fellow named Philippe, who was called upon to risk his life for the sake of his people.

Of course, Philippe didn't think of himself as anyone important—at least, not when he was growing up in the French countryside. He lived in a place called Noisy-le-Sec with his mother and father. They didn't seem like terribly important people, either—except, of course, to Philippe himself.

As far as young Philippe was concerned, he was just another kid. He learned his scholarly lessons. He did his chores. And he played in the surrounding woods every chance he got. Philippe never dreamed how quickly his simple, comfortable life could change.

Chapter Two

Laying his head on his front paws, Wishbone closed his eyes and imagined what it would be like to be Philippe, a simple young man with big things in store for him.

He saw himself sitting on a stone bench in his father's garden. A couple of months past his fifteenth birthday, Philippe was starting to become a man. He could tell because his clothes were getting small on him again and felt tight on his fur.

At the moment, he was looking at a series of mathematics problems he had scratched in the dirt with his paw. His parents had always insisted that he become an educated person, even though he would never be able to attend a great university.

"Let's see," he said out loud. "One hundred twenty-five divided by five . . . is twenty-five. One hundred fifty divided by six . . . is twenty-five as well. And . . ."

He never got to the third problem, because just then he heard his father cry out. Bunching his hind legs and leaping off his bench, he followed the cry toward the stone house where he had lived for as long as he could remember.

Philippe's four legs churned with great urgency. As he reached the house, however, he realized his father wasn't yelling anymore. From where he stood, he could see the old fellow through an open window.

Philippe's father was talking to Philippe's mother in sharp whispers. Obviously, they didn't want him to hear what they were saying, because he was the only other set of ears around. But Philippe had always been the curious sort, and he had the best hearing of anyone he knew. Hunkering down on his belly, he inched closer to listen in on their conversation.

His parents were talking about a letter. Judging from the tone of Philippe's father's voice, the letter was causing the poor man no end of anxiety. Pretty soon, his mother was upset as well.

"Are you sure?" Philippe's mother asked. "Did you see it there?"

"Without a doubt," his father replied. "Come, see for yourself!"

A moment later, Philippe's father ushered his mother out of their house. Then he brought her around to the back of the house. That was where they had a well that supplied them with drinking water.

Philippe followed them. However, he stayed out of sight. He was afraid that if they saw him, they would pretend there was nothing wrong. Then he would never find out what was upsetting them so.

His father pulled his mother over to the well. Then the two of them leaned over to peer down into its depths. Philippe's father groaned and wrung his hands, still unaware that his son was watching him.

"What will I tell Her Majesty the Queen?" he

asked. "Should I tell her a breeze came and blew her letter away? Should I say the wind caused the paper to float straight to the bottom of this well?"

"Isn't it the truth?" Philippe's mother replied.

"Of course it is," said his father. "But what if she doesn't believe me? What if she thinks I gave the letter to someone—one of her enemies, perhaps? Can you imagine what she would do to us then?"

"Yipes!" Philippe whispered to himself. "The queen . . . of France?"

Suddenly, he was as scared as his parents were. Why would the queen be writing letters to his father? And what information could be contained in such a letter that his parents might be endangered by its loss?

"We need to find a workman who can recover the letter," Philippe's father told his mother. "It has to be someone who can't read and realize it's from the queen. But who can we get?"

Philippe's mother came up with a name, and away they ran to fetch the man. As soon as they were gone, Philippe approached the well. Leaping up on its stone exterior, he looked inside it.

Sure enough, at the bottom of that deep, dank hole, there was a patch of white floating on the surface. Peering down as hard as he could, he saw it was a piece of paper with writing on it.

"The letter," he muttered. "If I can see what's in it, maybe I can figure out the link between my parents and the queen."

Philippe considered the stones that made up the well. They had loosened over the years and jutted out here and there. He had always been good at climbing rocks. With a little luck, he could get down into the well, fish out the letter, and climb back up again.

The idea of descending into such a dark, unfriendly place was a little scary to him. But in the end, he was more curious than frightened. He took a deep breath, then made his way down into the well.

Philippe went from one jutting stone to the other. He was careful to keep his paws steady on their slick, mossy surfaces. But as the rectangular shape of the letter got closer and closer, the circle of gray sky overhead, defined by the mouth of the well, got farther and farther away.

He could hear every scrape of his paws, magnified as the well echoed it back at him. It was damp down there. It was also colder than he had imagined—so cold, in fact, it cut right through his fur. He began to wonder what would happen if he fell in the water and there was no one around to get him out.

But that didn't stop him from his pursuit. He wanted desperately to know what was in the letter. So he kept at his mission, descending stone by stone, delving ever more deeply into the wet, drafty well.

Finally, Philippe got close enough to reach out and snatch the letter—which he did, with a swipe of his paw. Then he picked up the paper carefully in his mouth and started climbing back up the jagged stones.

Going up was even harder than going down. Philippe kept thinking his next step would be his last. But little by little, the circle of sky got bigger and bigger. Just when he thought the cold would sap the last of his strength, he took one final leap out onto the rim of the well.

"I made it!" he thought happily.

With the letter in his mouth, Philippe returned to

the stone bench in the garden. Then he laid the letter out flat on the bench. The words on the paper were smudged and faded by the well water, but he could still make them out.

As Philippe read, his eyes opened wider and wider, and wider still. He would never have dared to dream the kind of things he read in the queen's letter—for it was, indeed, from the queen.

Philippe was some kind of highborn nobleman, if the soggy letter could be believed. And his parents— the people who had raised him—weren't his natural parents at all. They were noble people themselves, though of a somewhat lower rank than Philippe.

A long time ago, the letter noted, Philippe had been given over to their care. His adoptive parents had raised him as if he were their own, it seemed. In time, they had come to love him. But in the beginning, they had taken him in only out of devotion to the queen.

Hearing noises, Philippe walked over to the bushes and peered through them. He could smell a new person nearby. He saw his parents and a workman standing around the well, scratching their heads.

"It's all wet here," the workman was saying, running his fingers along the rim of the well. "It looks as if someone climbed down inside already, and then climbed back out."

"How can that be?" Philippe's father asked. "Who could have . . . ?"

That was when he turned in the direction of the garden. His eyes met Philippe's, despite the tangle of bushes between them. And in that moment, both of them knew their lives would never be the same again.

"Philippe," said his father, "come here."

Naturally, Philippe did as he was told. Skirting the

bushes, he approached his father and sat. Then he waited patiently as his father began to pace. No doubt, the old man was trying to figure out what to say. Meanwhile, his mother returned to the house, and the workman left.

Philippe snorted. Some guys might have been happy to find out they were noblemen, with all kinds of privileges and maybe even a rich family somewhere. Not Philippe, though. He *liked* his simple life just the way it was.

Still, he was curious about his past. It was only natural to feel that way. He wanted to know where he had come from, and what he had left behind.

As he sat at his father's feet, Philippe saw how unhappy the man looked. Obviously, his father hadn't planned on this sudden turn of events.

Finally, Philippe couldn't contain his curiosity any longer. "So . . . you're not really my father," he said. "Are you?"

He realized now that he had suspected it all along, deep down inside. But until this moment, he had never really thought carefully about it.

The old man frowned and shook his head. "No, Philippe, I'm not your true father. But I love you as though you really were my son. And your mother loves you, as well, even though she's not your real mother."

Philippe wagged his tail. Now, he thought, they were getting somewhere. "So, if you don't mind my asking, who *are* my mother and father—the *real* ones, I mean?"

The old man sighed. "I can't tell you that, son. Perhaps it's better that you don't know."

"But why?" Philippe asked. "Surely, if the queen asked you to raise me and keep me safe all these years, she had big plans for me. What harm could it do to tell me about my true parents?"

His father shook his head. "Please, Philippe, do not press the matter. Just forget what you found out. It will be safer that way for everyone concerned—yourself, most of all."

With that, he left to go into the house. Philippe remained outside, to sit alone, his tail swishing back and fourth nervously. Unfortunately, he thought, the queen's letter had produced a lot more questions than answers.

Over the next few days, Philippe tried again and again to pry the details of his life out of his parents. But they turned him away every time, insisting he was better off not knowing.

Meanwhile, the queen's letter was returned to her, as Philippe's parents had agreed. His father wrote a note to go along with it, to explain how the letter had gotten wet. However, the note made no mention of Philippe's having seen the queen's letter.

Finally, Philippe took his father's advice and tried to forget about the letter. After all, he was happy, wasn't he? That was really all that mattered. If the queen had plans for him, big or small, he would certainly find out in due time.

A week or so after he had descended into the well, Philippe went to pick apples off the trees in his parents' orchard. The apples there were big and red and ripe that time of year, and he loved the slightly tart taste of them in his mouth.

As soon as he reached the orchard, however, he heard the sound of hoofbeats—in fact, a whole lot of hoofbeats. He turned around and looked back toward his parents' house.

"That's strange," he said to himself. "Our home is so far off the beaten track that we don't get very many visitors here. And when we do, they don't usually come in large groups."

Suddenly, Philippe had a bad feeling. A *very* bad feeling. It sent chills down his spine straight to the tip of his tail. Philippe sensed that he and his parents were in some kind of danger.

He ran back in the direction of his house as fast as his four legs could carry him. He hadn't gotten more than halfway home before a gloved hand reached out for him and yanked him off the path.

"Hey!" he cried out. "Get your mitts off me!"

Philippe found himself in the grip of someone much bigger and stronger than himself. The man wore dark clothes and a dark hat, so his face was not visible.

"Pick on someone your own size!" Philippe said.

The young nobleman fought with all his strength to free himself, scratching and clawing with all four paws and even snapping his teeth. However, he was unable to break the man's iron grasp.

Then a handful of other men appeared. They were also dressed in dark clothes and dark hats, just like the first one.

"I guess you all go to the same tailor," Philippe observed.

The men weren't amused. Before Philippe knew it, he was wrapped up tightly in a heavy black cloak. A moment later, a flowery-scented handkerchief was pressed against his snout.

Philippe began to get light-headed. As darkness closed in on him, he sensed this attack had something to do with the queen's letter. He wished now that he had left the silly thing floating in the well.

26

Chapter Three

Wishbone heard a loud *crack*.

It brought him to his feet, jolting him out of his daydream about Philippe and the men who had kidnapped him. He wasn't in seventeenth-century France anymore, he realized. He was on the baseball field with Joe and his friends David and Samantha.

Still, he was sure he had been dreaming for only a few minutes. Joe was still standing at home plate with a bat in his hands. Sam and David were still in the field.

As Wishbone watched, Samantha tossed the ball back to Joe. Joe caught it on one bounce with his bare hand.

"Okay," Wishbone said, scurrying to his place in the outfield. "Hit another one out here. I'm ready now."

Joe tossed the ball up in front of him and then hit a grounder to David. David snatched the ball up cleanly and threw it back to Joe.

But Joe was distracted again—no doubt by the kids on the next field. Instead of catching David's throw, he got hit in the knee by the ball. Wishbone cringed, fearing that Joe might have gotten hurt.

"Joe!" Samantha cried out.

Joe bent over and rubbed his knee. Luckily, he didn't seem to be in very much pain.

David ran in. "Are you all right?" he asked.

Joe nodded. "I'm fine. I just wasn't ready for the throw, that's all."

As Sam jogged in, too, David shook his head. "You weren't ready because you were looking at something else."

Joe didn't argue with him. He knew it was true.

On the other side of the park, the traveling team players were going through a fielding-and-throwing drill. Clearly, Joe wanted to be practicing with them, even if he didn't come right out and say so.

David sighed. "Come on," he said. "Let's go home."

Joe looked at him. "Home? Why?"

"Because you're not being much fun," his friend told him honestly. "You may be here with us, but your mind is somewhere else."

Joe winced. "Sorry."

"It's okay," said Sam. "Besides, I ought to get home anyway. I've got a book report due in a couple of days and I've got to get started on it."

Wishbone knew that Samantha was just being kind. He was certain she wanted to continue playing ball as much as David did. But she didn't want to force Joe to play if he had something else on his mind.

"Are you sure?" asked Joe.

"Positive," Sam assured him.

She picked up a bat and slung it over her shoulder. "Come on," she said. "Let's go."

Joe and David picked up the rest of their equipment. Together, they headed back for their houses.

But Wishbone didn't follow them—not right

away, at least. He saw something he wanted to investigate first.

Across the street, Damont had been observing Joe as he watched the traveling team players. Now that Joe was leaving the park, the Damonster crossed the street again. With Colby and Marcus trailing behind him, Damont headed straight for the kids on the next field.

The seventh-graders stopped their practice and gathered around Damont. Even with his super-sharp hearing, Wishbone couldn't make out what they were saying. Knowing Damont, however, Wishbone was sure the kid was up to no good.

Then he saw Damont pull some money out of his pocket. With a smile on his face, he handed it over to three of the boys in the blue uniforms.

"Uh-oh," Wishbone told himself. "Now I'm *sure* there's something fishy in the works. And being a dog, I hate fish."

Damont was clearly doing something underhanded—something that probably had to do with the election for class president. The terrier didn't know what it was yet. But as sure as his name was Wishbone, he promised himself he would find out.

First, however, he would head for home and a nice, tasty dinner. After all, he couldn't be a great detective on an empty stomach, could he?

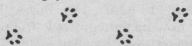

The next day, Joe and David walked to school together. Wishbone came along. He liked listening to their banter. And if he managed to chase a squirrel or two, that would be a bonus.

This particular morning, Officer Krulla passed them in his black-and-white squad car on his way to work. He grinned beneath his yellow-tinted glasses, and he waved to the boys. Then he waved to Wishbone, as well.

As they got closer to the school, Wishbone heard the sounds of other kids. They were laughing and whispering and arguing good-naturedly. But it was rare for one of them to shout.

So, when Wishbone heard a loud yell from across the street, he was quite surprised. He was even more surprised when he realized the person doing the yelling didn't look familiar.

He was a red-haired boy with green eyes and lots of freckles. Though Joe was big for his age, the boy was taller than Joe by a couple of inches. He wasn't alone, either. He had two other big guys with him.

As it happened, Joe hadn't yet pinpointed the source of the yell. Seeing that, the red-haired boy cupped his hands around his mouth and shouted again. "Hey, you! You—in the orange shirt!"

Finally, Joe glanced at the boy. Then he looked at his shirt—which was a very definite shade of orange. Then he turned to the boy again.

"Who? Me?" he shouted back.

"Yeah, you," the redhead replied.

Suddenly, Wishbone knew who the stranger was. The terrier hadn't recognized the boy without his blue uniform, but now he remembered. The redhead was a member of the traveling baseball team.

Wishbone recalled the sight of Damont handing out money to the red-haired kid and his two companions. The dog's tail wagged with anticipation, wondering what the boy wanted from Joe.

"Stay there a second," the redhead told Wishbone's pal. "We want to talk to you, okay?"

Joe looked at David. David shrugged.

"Might as well see what he wants," David said.

He and Joe waited for the older boys to catch up with them. Wishbone waited, too, eager to find out what was going on. After all, if the trio was in cahoots with Damont, it wasn't exactly a great character endorsement.

"My name's Ted," said the red-haired boy. He held out his hand as he caught up with Joe and David. "Ted McIntyre, that is. But my friends call me Red."

Joe took Red's hand and shook it. "Joe Talbot. And this," he continued, indicating his friend with a gesture, "is David Barnes."

"Nice to meetcha," said Red.

He introduced his buddies as "Flip" Gomez and "Lefty" Hayes. One at a time, they pumped Joe's hand. They shook hands with David, too, but it seemed to Wishbone they were looking at Joe the whole time.

"Y'know," said Red, "I've been watching you." He turned to Flip and Lefty. "In fact, we all have."

"Watching you play, that is," said Lefty. "And you look pretty good."

"I do?" said Joe.

"For a sixth-grader," Red told him, "you look great. That's why we're going to give you a shot—that is, if you want it."

"A shot?" Joe echoed.

"At making the team," Flip explained. "You know, the *traveling* team."

"Are ya interested?" asked Red.

Joe's eyes almost popped out of his head. "Interested? You bet I am."

Red nodded. "I had a feeling you'd say that." He looked Joe in the eye. "So, tell me . . . have ya ever played catcher?"

Joe thought for a moment. "A little," he said.

"Like it?" asked Red.

"Sure," said Joe. "I like playing just about any position."

Red nodded. "That's good, 'cause a catcher's about the only thing we really need." He paused for a second. "Tell ya what—we're having a practice in the park Saturday morning. That's tomorrow. No coach or anything, just the players. Why don'cha come on down and try out?"

"Er . . . okay," Joe replied. "But . . . I mean, I don't know if I can dig up a catcher's mask and everything."

The redhead dismissed the problem with a wave of his hand. "Don't worry about it. We've got all the equipment you'll need."

Joe smiled. "Gee . . . thanks." He turned to David. "This is great."

David glanced at the older boys. "Yeah," he said, "great." But he didn't sound half as enthusiastic as Joe.

Wishbone was surprised. After he saw Red and his friends taking money from Damont, he had believed the older boys would try immediately to stop Joe from running seriously against Damont.

But they hadn't—at least, not as far as Wishbone could tell. Of course, that didn't mean they weren't up to *something*.

It just meant he hadn't figured it out yet.

Wishbone wished he could tell Joe what Damont was up to. He wished he could keep his closest pal from walking into the trap he knew was being set for him.

But for the time being, all he could do was grab Joe's pants leg in his teeth and attempt to pull him away from the older boys. So that was exactly what he did—though he wasn't able to pull his buddy very far.

"Wishbone!" Joe chuckled. "What are you doing, boy?" He looked at Red and shrugged helplessly. "I've never seen him act like this. I don't know what's gotten into him."

Red laughed. "It's okay. See ya tomorrow—say, around eight-thirty?"

"I'll be there," Joe promised him.

The older boys nodded and then walked away, leaving Joe with David and Wishbone. As soon as Red and the others were gone, the terrier released his hold on Joe's pants leg.

Joe looked at Wishbone. "What was that all about?"

"He doesn't like Red and his friends," David told him, as if he knew it for a fact. "And to tell you the truth, neither do I."

Joe glanced at the retreating figures of the seventh-graders. "I don't know. They seemed like pretty good guys to me."

"Maybe you weren't looking hard enough," David suggested. "There's something about those guys I don't trust."

"You know what your problem is?" Joe asked him. "You're too suspicious." He clapped David on the shoulder. "C'mon. If we're late for school, I won't get a chance to sign up for the election."

As Wishbone watched them go, he shook his head. "No wonder they call a catcher's gear the tools of ignorance. Joe doesn't have a clue."

Unfortunately, as much as Wishbone didn't want to admit it, *he* didn't have a clue, either. He was sure that Red and the others were going to try to keep Joe from running for president—he just didn't know how.

But that would change, Wishbone promised himself. With a little canine ingenuity, he would find out what Damont's scheme was and then blow it wide open. . . .

All that day, the terrier kept his eyes and ears open—but he didn't make any progress in his investigation. He was still pondering the problem that night as he curled up at the foot of Joe's bed and yawned sleepily.

Again, he thought of Philippe, the main character in *The Man in the Iron Mask*. Like Joe, Philippe had been tossed about by forces he didn't understand.

Of course, Philippe had a much worse situation than Joe does. The men who abducted Philippe didn't take him anywhere as nice as a baseball field. They threw him in prison—*an awful place called the Bastille.*

Once again, Wishbone imagined that he was Philippe. But he was no longer a young lad. Now he was a twenty-three-year-old adult. . . .

Chapter Four

It wasn't bad enough that Philippe was in a dank, depressing cell—the same one where he had spent the last eight years of his life. It wasn't bad enough he had no one to talk to, and only the tiniest window to give some light to his otherwise cheerless days.

To add to his misery, he was forced to wear a heavy, bulky iron muzzle all the time. The cold, clammy contraption scraped against his fur and prevented anyone from seeing his features.

I'll bet they're nice features, too, Philippe thought. *For all I know, I could be a really handsome guy. But, with this mask on me, no one can say for sure. Not even me, because I've never gotten a good look at myself.*

Mirrors, after all, were expensive items, owned only by the rich. Most everyone else saw their reflections only in clear lakes or slow-running streams, but the grounds around the house where Philippe grew up had neither of those things.

"Boy," he said out loud, "how I miss my parents' place. What I wouldn't give to be romping through the fields again the way I used to, chasing cats and rolling in clover. Now, *that* was the life."

If Philippe closed his eyes, he could picture himself stretched out on the stone bench in the garden, having a peaceful nap. He could hear birds singing in the trees. He could taste the pungent apples that grew in his father's orchard. And he could feel the sun caressing his fur, warm and welcome.

But when he opened his eyes, he came back to the harsh reality of life in his jail cell, with nothing to look forward to. All he got every day was a crust of bread and a tin mug full of warm water. It was enough to make someone lose his mind.

"And what have I done to deserve this loneliness and deprivation?" Philippe asked himself. "What crime have I committed?"

He guessed it had something to do with the queen's letter—the one that had fallen into the well. But no one would tell him for sure.

Nobody would tell him what had happened to his parents, either. Of course, the fact that they hadn't come to visit him in prison wasn't a very good sign. For all he knew, they had been sent to prison, as well . . . or maybe even been killed by the men who had abducted him.

As far as Philippe knew, his parents had been innocent of any wrongdoing—as innocent as Philippe himself. But that didn't seem to matter. It was still his fate to waste away in a chilly, rat-infested prison, cut off from the wonderful world he had known.

"Life isn't very fair sometimes," Philippe said aloud.

"No," replied a voice. "It isn't."

Philippe turned to his cell door, surprised by the response. Pressing his masked face against the little barred square in the door, he peered into the darkness beyond his cell.

"Is there someone out there?" he asked.

"There is, indeed," came the answer.

Someone struck a match, making the prisoner flinch. After all, he didn't see too many bright lights in his cell. After a while, however, he could see a candle. Then, as his eyes adjusted further, he could make out a human form behind the candle flame.

It wasn't his jailer, either. His jailer was considerably shorter than this fellow. In any case, he knew his jailer's scent, and this person had the scent of someone new.

Philippe's visitor stood tall and straight. He had gray eyes, blond hair, and the bearing of a nobleman. His goatee and moustache were neatly trimmed, and he wore some very fancy clothes.

"Who are you?" Philippe asked, his voice muffled by the mask he wore.

"My name is Aramis," his visitor informed him.

"I've heard that name only once before," Philippe said. "There was an Aramis who became famous throughout France as one of the Three Musketeers— the heroic group of guards who defended the king against all manner of danger and deceit."

The stranger smiled grimly. "At your service, my friend."

"That's you?" asked Philippe. "The legendary musketeer? Standing right outside my cell? Wow!"

"It is I," Aramis replied, "in the flesh. But I didn't come here to talk about *me*."

"I believe you," said Philippe.

If someone as famous as Aramis had come to see him, there was obviously something big going on. But the prisoner had no idea what it might be.

Michael Jan Friedman

"So why *are* you here?" Philippe asked.

"Before I answer your question," his visitor said, "allow me to ask a few of my own. I would appreciate it if you would reply as truthfully as you can."

"I'd be happy to do so," Philippe told the bearded man. "But I must say, I can't imagine what good your questions will do you. I'm a prisoner, as you can see. If I ever knew anything worth knowing, I've probably forgotten it."

"Let me be the judge of that," Aramis replied.

The prisoner nodded. "Very well. By all means, begin."

"You were raised on a farm?"

"Yes," said Philippe. "In a place called Noisy-le-Sec."

"By a man and a woman whom you understood to be your parents?"

"Yes," the prisoner agreed again. "Though, of course, they weren't that at all, as I later discovered."

"We will get to that soon enough," Aramis assured him. "Tell me . . . did your father ever give you any special advice?"

This bearded man was rather nosy, Philippe thought. And he wasn't even a bloodhound.

"My father used to have a saying—that a man was bound to make for himself in the world what Heaven had refused him at birth."

"And what did that mean to you?" asked Aramis.

Cocking his head to one side, Philippe thought for a moment. "That I would have to depend on myself for my livelihood, since my parents could offer me no great inheritance."

"I see," said his visitor. "Now, tell me something else. How much do you recall of your childhood?"

"Not as much as I used to," the prisoner told him.

"Do you remember a woman who came to see you when you were very little? A very well-to-do woman? A lady of beautiful and majestic bearing, with a high forehead and deep blue eyes?"

As Philippe tried to picture this person, the years seemed to melt away. He could see the woman as if she were standing there right in front of him.

"Why, yes," he answered, surprised. "I *do* remember her."

"She came every month, did she not? In a handsome carriage?"

The prisoner looked at him. "Yes . . . but how do you know that?"

"I was a musketeer, remember? Now," said Aramis, "tell me this: Do you remember this woman sitting on a stone bench in your parents' garden? Do you remember her speaking with them there?"

Philippe swallowed. "Is there *anything* you don't know?"

Aramis ignored the comment. "And when you looked at her, my young friend, was she smiling at you? But not in a happy way, perhaps? In fact, might it be said she seemed sad as she looked at you with those blue eyes of hers, as if she felt sorry for something that had happened to you?"

Philippe remembered. "It's true," he said.

At the time, he had wondered what there was for her to feel sorry about. After all, he had been pleased with his plain, country life.

Still, the lady's smile had always been sad when she looked at him. He had always wondered about that after she left.

Unfortunately, as Philippe had grown older, the

lady's visits stopped. He had asked his parents why the lady no longer came to see the family. They told Philippe that the situation was nothing he needed to concern himself with—it was a business matter, that was all.

"More recently," said Aramis, "when you were fifteen or so, you found a letter in a peculiar place."

Philippe tilted his head. "You must be a mind-reader."

"Was there a letter?" his visitor insisted.

"Yes. There was a letter."

"And where did you see it?" Aramis asked.

Philippe sighed. "At the bottom of a well, floating in the water."

"You were curious about this letter," his visitor noted.

"Yes, very curious. I fished it out of the well. Fortunately, it wasn't so soggy that the ink had dissolved."

"You could still read it," said Aramis.

"Yes," Philippe confirmed. "In fact, I did."

"And what did it say?"

The prisoner looked around, to make sure no one else was listening. "You're going to think I'm crazy," he replied, "but it said I was under the protection of the queen—the queen of France, that is."

Philippe had expected Aramis to laugh at the notion. But he wasn't laughing. In fact, the man looked as serious as ever.

"You don't believe you were under the queen's protection?"

The prisoner rolled his eyes. "Come on, now. If the queen were my protector, why would I be rotting here in a prison cell?"

Aramis didn't answer. "Then what?" he asked instead.

Philippe shrugged. "A couple of weeks later, a bunch of men showed up and kidnapped me. Before I knew it, they had put me in this prison—even though I hadn't done anything wrong."

"You read the letter," his visitor noted.

"Since when is it a crime to read a letter?" Philippe asked.

"That depends on what's in the letter," Aramis pointed out wisely, "and it also depends on who's doing the reading."

"Mon dieu!" exclaimed the prisoner. "How would they have punished me if I'd chewed it up, as well?"

Aramis stroked his neatly trimmed beard. "You've been good enough to answer all my questions. Now, let me tell you a little story. I think you'll find it most educational."

"I'd prefer it if you'd sneak me a key," Philippe suggested.

"The story first," his visitor said. "Then we'll see about the key."

He leaned closer to the barred square in the cell door. His eyes twinkled in the candlelight.

"Twenty-three years ago," he said, "almost to the day, the king and queen of France experienced a joyous event. It was the birth of a son who could carry on the family name and become king when his father died. But, you see, there was more than one son born to the royal family that day. In fact, the queen gave birth to twins."

Philippe stared at him. *"Twins,* you say?"

Aramis nodded. "That event presented a small problem. You see, the older of the boys would become

41

king. That much was certain. But the king was afraid that the younger twin would become jealous one day and challenge his brother's claim to the throne. That would result in a civil war, from which France might never recover."

The prisoner was starting to see where his visitor was going with this story—as incredible as it might seem. "So the second son was kept a secret. That's what you're suggesting, isn't it?"

"Exactly. He was sent away, to live with a couple in the countryside. But his birth mother couldn't bear the thought of not seeing him grow up. So she sneaked away from the royal household once a month and went to the farm where her other son lived. While she was there, she would sit on a stone bench and look at him sadly, because she knew she could never publicly claim him as her own."

Philippe gulped. "The woman who visited me in my childhood . . ."

". . . was the same one who wrote the letter to your adoptive parents. In both cases," said Aramis, "it was the queen of France."

Philippe's eyes opened wide and his ears twitched. "And that second son, the prince's twin—"

"—is *you*," Aramis told him.

"I'm a prince?" the prisoner gasped.

"That's right."

"The brother of King Louis?"

"Absolutely," said Aramis.

"So the queen's *letter* . . . was about the queen's *litter?*"

"In a manner of speaking, yes."

"Wait a moment," Philippe demanded, finding it hard to catch his breath.

He was dizzy from all Aramis had said to him. Suddenly he felt his four legs threatening to buckle under him. He had imagined that something big was afoot, but this news was bigger than anything he'd been prepared for.

After all, it wasn't every day that someone told him he was a prince of France.

Then Philippe's better judgment began to take hold. He found himself doubting the bearded man's word.

"If I'm a prince," he asked, "what am I doing in this dirty cell? This place isn't fit for a cat, let alone a person of royal birth."

His visitor smiled grimly. "It's your royal birth that landed you here, my friend. Don't you see? Once you knew who you were—or at least suspected it—you were yet again a danger to your twin brother. And though he couldn't bring himself to kill his own flesh and blood, he couldn't let you become a threat to him and his reign, either."

Philippe shook his head. It seemed unbelievable to him that anyone could be so cruel.

"My own brother did this to me?" he asked. "He had me thrown into a prison cell, to rot for the past eight years? Put an itchy, uncomfortable mask on me?"

"Yes," said Aramis. "Otherwise, one of your jailers might have seen you and noticed your resemblance to the king. Then the truth might have come out."

The prisoner considered what his visitor had said. Then he shook his head. "I was born at night," he quipped, "but it wasn't *last* night. I mean, don't get me wrong, this is a very entertaining story, and a guy in my position doesn't get to hear too many stories. But me . . . the prince of France? *Me?*"

"You don't believe me?" asked Aramis.

"Well," said Philippe, not wishing to offend the man, "let's just say it smells fishy. And I have an excellent sense of smell."

"Despite the letter from the queen?"

"Circumstantial evidence," Philippe replied.

"Then you leave me no choice," said his visitor.

"No choice?" the prisoner echoed. He didn't like the sound of that.

"No choice," Aramis explained, "but to prove what I say is true."

With that, he took something out of his tunic. Philippe could see by the candle's light that it was a key. His visitor handed it to him.

"Here," he said. "This will unlock your mask."

"Really?" Philippe asked.

"Really," Aramis confirmed. He looked over his shoulder, into the shadows of the prison. "Just hurry."

The prisoner hurried, all right. Just as his visitor had said, the key unlocked his mask. Gingerly, he removed it, feeling a sense of freedom he hadn't known for years.

His head moved from side to side on its own. It was as if a great weight had been lifted from him. Philippe felt like leaping up in the air and doing somersaults. He felt like howling his happiness at the top of his lungs to anyone who would listen.

But he didn't, of course. He didn't want to attract any attention, after all.

Then Aramis took something else out of his tunic. This time, he produced a small mirror. He slipped it to Philippe through the bars.

Understanding what his visitor meant for him to

do, the prisoner turned his back to the candle flame and looked at himself in the reflective glass. For the first time in his life, he saw his own face clearly. He saw the brown patch around one eye and the spots that covered one ear.

And he gasped.

Philippe had seen King Louis a thousand times—though never in person. After all, his jailer walked by his door several times a day carrying a lighted candle in one hand and a coin bearing the king's image in the other. The jailer had a habit of flipping the coin in the air and referring to it as a "louis."

"You see?" said Aramis. "You're a dead ringer for King Louis."

The prisoner looked at him. "Do me a favor and leave the 'dead' part out."

"As you wish," his visitor replied. "In any case, you can see I wasn't lying to you. You bear a remarkable resemblance to the king—the kind only his own blood could bear."

Philippe looked at himself in the mirror again. "It's hard to argue with that," he admitted.

"That extraordinary resemblance gives you a unique opportunity," said Aramis, "a unique opportunity, indeed." He leaned closer to the opening in the cell door and spoke more softly. "There are those who would like to see you on the throne of France, my friend. I admit, I am one of them. With a little doing, we could make that desire a reality."

The prisoner stared at him. "Make me . . . king? It's a ridiculous idea."

His visitor shook his head. "Louis doesn't seem to think so, or he would never have imprisoned you. For years, those who knew of your birth have feared

46

you would seek the throne. Would they have felt this fear if the possibility were, as you say, ridiculous?"

Philippe thought for a moment. "Maybe not." He looked around his cell. "But how can I—?"

"How can you become king when you're a prisoner here?" Aramis interrupted. "Leave that to me. In fact, leave everything to me." His eyes crinkled at the corners. "Imagine, king of all France. And you have but to say the word."

The prisoner didn't think it would be as easy to become king as his visitor suggested. But before he could even consider it, there was something else he had to know.

"Why are you doing all this?" Philippe asked. "How do you hope to benefit from placing me on the throne? And as a former musketeer, shouldn't you be *serving* the current king instead of plotting against him?"

A shadow seemed to pass over the face of Aramis. "I served your father, King Louis the Thirteenth," he answered. "*This* King Louis—the Fourteenth, your twin—is nothing but a spoiled child. He is a man more devoted to fancy parties and extravagant clothes than he is to governing his royal subjects. Slowly but surely, he is draining France's treasury dry. If he is allowed to continue to rule, France will fall into serious debt, leaving her helpless to defend herself against neighboring countries."

"And you think I would do better?" the prisoner wondered.

Aramis smiled a grim smile. "I know you would. You were raised on simple, wholesome country virtues, Philippe. You learned what it meant to work hard, and to be thrifty with your money. Above all, you learned to deal fairly with people."

The prisoner had to admit all that Aramis said was

true. Along with the mathematics and history he had learned, he had been taught to treat all people with dignity and respect.

Aramis shook his head sadly. "King Louis, on the other hand, is always taking advantage of his authority and power. He changes the laws whenever he feels like it. He arrests anyone who opposes him. Sometimes, he puts people in jail just so he can take over their personal property—that is, if they have some bauble he's come to admire."

Philippe grunted. "I guess you'd say my brother, Louis, doesn't play well with others."

"That would be an understatement," his visitor told him. "Only by replacing him can France have any hope of survival."

The prisoner paced in his cell, feeling its hard floor under his paws. "I don't know, Aramis. I mean, sure, I'd like to get out of prison. And I'm as patriotic as the next Frenchman . . . I even like french fries. But I don't know if I can handle royal politics. You said it yourself—I'm a country boy. I like to dig into real dirt, not into dirty politics."

"But you are a country boy with royal blood in his veins," his visitor reminded him. "I assure you, that fact will make all the difference."

Philippe wished he were as confident as Aramis. He wished he could see where his visitor's plan would end—and whether, in the long run, it would help France or hurt her.

But no one could see the future—not even Aramis, who seemed to know everything else. "I need time to think," Philippe said.

Aramis was disappointed. It showed in his face. But he didn't argue with Philippe's decision.

"Take all the time you need," he said softly.

Then he pointed to the mask in the prisoner's hands. Philippe looked at it. It was an ugly thing—the ugliest thing he could imagine.

"Forgive me," his visitor said, "but we must restore your mask to its customary place. Otherwise, the warden of the prison will wonder with whom you spoke, and how that someone managed to obtain a certain key. Perhaps he will also be curious why you resemble the king of France."

Philippe nodded. "I understand."

Reluctantly, he put the mask back on and locked it into place. He shuddered at the cold, hard feel of it on his fur. Then he returned the key to Aramis. Instantly, Philippe missed the feeling of freedom that he'd tasted all too briefly.

The mask was like a prison within a prison. It seemed to close him off from the world in a way no cell ever could.

"I'll come back," his visitor assured him. "For your answer." Then he vanished into the darkness outside Philippe's cell.

The prisoner lay down on the floor. He was scared and excited at the same time. Suddenly, he had a lot to think about.

In fact, he tossed and turned all night, wondering what he should do. In the morning, when the first rays of the sun slanted through his window, he was still painfully undecided.

Chapter Five

"Wait a minute," Wishbone said, looking around him at the brightly lit room. "This is an awful lot of sunlight for one tiny prison window."

Then he remembered. He wasn't in a cell after all. He was in Joe's bedroom, curled up at the foot of his friend's bed.

Just then, Joe woke up and glanced with sleepy eyes at his alarm clock. It seemed Joe hadn't slept well the night before. Like Philippe, he must have been too excited.

But Wishbone didn't think any amount of fatigue was going to stop Joe from meeting Red at the ball field. A moment later, he was proven right—as Joe tossed off his covers and bolted out of bed.

After he dressed quickly and grabbed his baseball mitt, Joe ran downstairs. He poured himself a glass of orange juice and downed it faster than he should have. Finally, he scrawled a note to his mom, left it on the kitchen table, and ran out the door.

Wishbone was right on his heels. "Hey, slow down," the terrier said. "What's your hurry?"

But he knew only too well what Joe's hurry was. The boy was on the verge of fulfilling a lifelong dream. If he played well enough, he would make the traveling team.

With Wishbone right behind him, Joe made it to the ball field in record time. The kids in the blue uniforms were just starting to pull their equipment out of their bags.

As Wishbone watched, Red put his arm around Joe. Then he introduced him to the rest of the team.

A few of the seventh-graders seemed surprised that Joe had been allowed to try out. But Ted dismissed them with a wave of his hand.

"It's okay," he said, "really. I cleared it myself."

"Yeah," Flip chimed in. "I'm a witness."

The other players seemed to be satisfied. After all, they were there to play ball, not to kick anyone off the field.

Wishbone lowered himself to the warm, sunlit ground behind the backstop and took a whiff of the freshly cut grass. But he couldn't enjoy the warmth of the ground or the sweetness of the smell—not when he knew Joe was being bamboozled somehow.

As Red had promised, Joe was given a catcher's mask and a set of protective pads. The team didn't have a catcher's mitt handy, however, so Joe had to use his outfielder's model.

He didn't seem to mind, though. He was just thrilled to be part of the action.

When the practice started, Joe was behind home plate. A kid named Stretch Merkle did the pitching. The other players took turns at bat. When they weren't hitting, they took positions in the field.

Joe did his usual good job on defense. He caught a

couple of high pops in front of home plate. He even dove to snatch a foul ball before it could hit the ground.

A little more than half the team had come up to hit when Wishbone heard Joe's name being called. Raising his head, he looked in the direction the shouts had come from.

His tail began to wag when he saw it was David and Samantha, walking over from the next field. To Wishbone's discerning eye, it looked as if they had something on their minds.

Impatient to know what it was, Wishbone skirted the wire backstop and scooted across the infield. When he got to the outfield and the nice, soft grass, he ran even quicker.

Okay, he thought, as he pulled up in front of Joe's friends in a cloud of loose grass cuttings. *What's up, guys? What's the good word?*

David and Samantha barely seemed to notice him. Apparently, they were too intent on their conversation to think about much else.

"Wednesday doesn't give Joe much time," Samantha said.

"Joe'll be ready," David assured her. "Just wait and see."

By that time, Joe had begun jogging out to meet them. He was already on the outfield grass.

"Ready for what?" Wishbone wondered. "What's happening on Wednesday?" Unfortunately, he was going to have to wait to find out.

"Hi," said Joe, coming to a halt in front of his friends.

He glanced back over his shoulder at the kids he'd been playing with, then took off his mask. His face was red with exertion.

"I can't talk too long," he told Sam and David, brushing aside a sweaty lock of hair. "I don't want to miss any of the practice."

"Damont's challenged you to a debate," Samantha explained. "And it's on Wednesday. That doesn't give us much of a chance to get you ready."

"But you can bet *Damont* is going to be ready," said David.

Sam put her hand on Joe's shoulder. "You'd better set aside every spare moment between now and then. Debates are often the way elections are either won or lost."

Joe's brow wrinkled. "Every spare moment? But . . . I can't."

David tilted his head. "Why not?"

Joe jerked his thumb over his shoulder, indicating the players on the traveling team. "Red told me the catching job's as good as mine. But we've got a practice tomorrow, and then again on Monday and Tuesday." He shrugged. "And I'm going to have homework, too."

Samantha sighed. "That doesn't leave much time to prepare for the debate."

"No," David said in a disappointed tone of voice. "It doesn't leave much time at all."

"Maybe I could get Damont to reschedule the debate," Samantha suggested.

Joe shook his head. "It doesn't matter. We're going to have practices every day. Red said so." He looked at his friends. "Sorry, guys."

Sam looked disappointed as well. "You made a commitment, Joe. You signed up to run against Damont."

"And no one else did," David added. "When they heard you were running, they figured the school would be in good hands."

"And now the deadline's passed for anyone to sign up," said Sam. "So if you don't run, Damont really *will* run unopposed."

"Damont's been putting up his posters all over town," David said. "It's getting really obnoxious. I even saw him put one on the back of a little kid's tricycle. Believe me, the kid wasn't too thrilled about it."

Joe grunted. "I guess I wouldn't have been thrilled either."

"Joe," Wishbone said, "you've got to think about this decision some more."

David held his hands out in an appeal to Joe. "If you don't run against Damont, he's going to win hands down. It'll be the worst thing that ever happened to the school."

"Damont's hard enough to take as it is," Wishbone said. "Imagine what he'll be like if he gets himself elected class president."

Joe went silent for a moment. Then he shook his head. "I wish I could tear myself in two," he said at last, "but I can't. I've got to do one thing or the other. Right now, I can't think of anything I'd rather do than make the team." He paused. "You guys are my friends. You understand, don't you?"

David and Sam looked at each other. They both knew how much it meant to their friend to become a member of the traveling team.

"I guess so," Samantha said at last.

But neither she nor David was very happy with Joe's decision. Wishbone would have seen that even if he weren't a great detective.

"Hey, Joe!" Flip called out from the infield. He tossed the ball up in the air and caught it in his glove. "What's the holdup?"

"Nothing," Joe called back. "I'll be right there." He smiled at David and Samantha. "I'll see you two later, okay?"

"Okay," Sam said, speaking for both herself and David. But there wasn't a lot of enthusiasm in her voice.

Joe turned and jogged back to the baseball field. Halfway there, he slipped his catcher's mask back over his face.

"I'm back!" he yelled to Red and the other guys, long before he had actually returned to the diamond.

Suddenly, Wishbone realized what Damont had been up to all along. "Why didn't I see it before?" he asked himself.

Red and the others had enticed Joe to try out for the traveling team so that he wouldn't have time to prepare for the debate. And if he couldn't prepare for the debate, then he obviously couldn't run against Damont.

And Damont would win the election.

Wishbone ground his teeth together. *That Damont!* he thought angrily. *If there's ever a slippery angle to any situation, he'll find it!*

"Well," said David, as he watched Joe return to the baseball field, "that conversation could have gone better."

"You can say that again," Samantha replied.

The two of them began to walk away from the baseball field.

Wishbone turned to his unsuspecting pal. "Aw, Joe," he said, "can't you see what's going on?"

The terrier blew air through his nose. He was as unhappy as David and Samantha were. It was a sorry state of affairs, all right.

"But if there's a way to set it right," he vowed, "I'll find it."

After all, Wishbone wasn't just a cute little dog with one brown ear any longer—he was a cute little dog with one brown ear and a mission.

The traveling team's practice wasn't over for a couple of hours. By the time Joe and Wishbone walked into Joe's house, Joe's mother was almost ready to put lunch on the table.

Wishbone had recognized the intoxicating aroma of franks and beans all the way down the block. Now that he was actually standing there in the kitchen, he couldn't help but lick his chops in eager anticipation of what was to come.

"Gotta love it," he said.

Of course, the franks and beans were technically *Joe's* lunch. However, Wishbone knew he would get his share of the mouth-watering morsels. The kid was good that way.

Together, Wishbone and Joe's mom had done quite a job with the boy. Joe was one of the nicest, warmest, most understanding young people around. That was what made it so hard for Wishbone to watch Joe head for a fall.

"Go wash your hands," Ellen said.

"I'm on my way," Joe replied as he ran by her.

"Say," said Ellen, craning her neck to get a better look at Joe, "where did that mask come from?"

"The guys lent it to me," he explained. He laid down his glove and the mask outside the bathroom.

"The guys?" his mom wondered out loud.

"The guys on the traveling team," Joe explained from inside the bathroom.

Ellen smiled. "Are you trying out?" she asked.

"Good question," Wishbone said. "Ask another one. Maybe if you keep asking, you'll find out what's going on."

Joe came out of the bathroom, his hands still a little damp—but clean. "Actually, Red says I'm already on the team. He tells me I'm going to play catcher." He shrugged. "That's why I've got the mask."

"Come on, Ellen," Wishbone said. "Ask Joe about Damont. Ask him about the election for class president."

But Joe's mom just winked at her son. "Good for you, Joe. Now, sit down and eat before your food gets cold. A guy on the traveling team needs his strength, you know."

Joe smiled, too. "Yeah," he said. "I know." He proceeded to dig into his lunch.

Wishbone looked at Joe, then at Ellen, then at Joe again. He sighed and covered his face with his paws. It had been too much of a long shot to expect Ellen to get to the bottom of Joe's predicament.

After all, she hadn't seen Damont offer money to Red and the others. She didn't know Damont had anything to do with the situation at all.

If someone was going to save Joe, it would have to be Wishbone. But how? What could he do to slam the brakes on Damont's scheme?

Chapter Six

Back in the prison where Philippe was being held captive, the outlook was pretty gloomy as well.

It had been weeks since the prisoner had seen his new friend, Aramis. Philippe had begun to doubt whether the man with the beard was coming back again, as he had promised.

Then, late one evening, the prisoner heard a familiar voice outside his cell. "It is I, Your Majesty."

Leaping to his feet, Philippe pressed his face against the barred hole in his door. Sure enough, it was Aramis standing there. This time, he didn't have a candle in his hand.

A moment later, the prisoner heard a key turn in a lock. Wonder of wonders, the door to his cell creaked open.

"Come," the former musketeer said, waving for Philippe to follow him. "We must hurry, my prince."

Philippe hesitated for a moment. After all, he had been a prisoner in that cell for eight long years. The very thought of instant freedom took a little getting used to.

But not that *much,* he thought.

He ran after Aramis as quickly as his four legs would carry him. His mysterious friend led him through a dark, twisting hallway, then up a flight of slippery, stone stairs. Finally, the two of them came out into a courtyard.

A carriage was waiting for them there. The two horses hitched to the front of it were snorting noisily, clopping their hooves on the cobblestones beneath them. There was a driver, too—a big fellow, it seemed, doing his best to keep the beasts quiet.

Without a word to the driver, Aramis opened the door for Philippe, who pushed hard with his rear legs and leaped into the carriage. Then Aramis climbed in after Philippe and knocked a couple of times on the carriage's wooden door.

With that signal, the carriage began to move. Looking out through his window, Philippe saw they were headed for the far end of the prison courtyard. A pair of uniformed guards was waiting for them there, standing on either side of a huge, dark iron gate.

"Sink back into the seat as far as you can," Aramis told Philippe. Then he covered him with a cloak. "It won't make this any easier if the guards see that mask of yours."

Philippe did as he was told—he leaned back as far as he could. With the cloak over his face, he couldn't see what the guards' reaction was. But he could still hear their conversation with Aramis.

"As you can see," said the bearded man, "this letter explains everything. I suggest you read it quickly if you value your jobs—and your lives."

One of the guards gasped. Then he told the other one everything was in order. Seconds later, the carriage began to move forward again. Before long, Philippe and his friends were rattling over cobblestones outside the prison gate at an almost reckless pace.

"Here," Aramis told Philippe, whisking off his cloak. "We no longer have such a desperate need for concealment."

Philippe looked out at a dark, deserted street. Sticking his head out the window, he turned and gazed at the gray shape of the prison he had left behind. In one sense, however, he was still very much a prisoner.

He still wore the mask, after all. Until he got rid of that, too, he would never really feel free.

Pulling his head back inside, he turned to Aramis. "I don't suppose you might have that key you brought the other day—you know, the one that fits the lock of my mask?"

Aramis smiled. "I do, indeed."

Reaching into his vest, he pulled it out. Then he placed it in the lock and opened the mask. Gingerly, Philippe removed the heavy object.

He could feel the caress of the wind on his fur, cool and fresh after the sweaty closeness of the iron mask. It had been eight miserable years since Philippe had experienced anything like it—and what a glorious feeling it was!

"Thank you," he told the former musketeer.

"You're most welcome, Your Majesty," said Aramis.

"But . . . how did you manage to obtain my release?" Philippe asked, burning with curiosity.

Aramis sat back in his seat and twisted the end of his moustache. "I had dinner with the warden of the prison."

Philippe looked at him. "You're friends with him?"

His companion shrugged. "I wouldn't go so far

as to say *that*. But we have a number of friends in common."

"And you talked him into letting me go?"

Aramis shook his head. "I have a silver tongue, my friend, but even I could not have done that." He reached into his vest and took out a piece of paper with writing on it. "At least, not without this letter from the king."

He handed the letter to Philippe, who read it. He couldn't believe his eyes. "This is a letter calling for my release," he said, surprised. "But why would the king . . . ?"

"Why would he have you released," Aramis finished for him, "when he was the one who had you put there in the first place?"

"Yes," said Philippe. "Why?"

His friend chuckled. "Simple. The king's signature is a forgery."

"Then it wasn't Louis who signed it?"

"That's correct," said Aramis. "It was someone else entirely. A friend of mine is rather good at such things."

"You have some interesting friends," Philippe noted.

"I do at that," Aramis agreed. "In any case, even with the letter, the warden was reluctant to release you. However, one does not question a direct order from the king. When I reminded him of that, he turned pale and handed you over to me."

"I don't know what to say," Philippe told him. "Except for my parents' raising me, this is the kindest thing anyone has ever done for me."

Aramis smiled. "Think nothing of it." A moment later, his smile faded. "I have bad news about your parents."

Suddenly, Philippe felt a lump in his throat. He swallowed hard. "They're dead, aren't they?"

His friend nodded sadly. "They were killed by the king's men the very day you were abducted."

Philippe hung his head, heaved a sigh, and felt his tail droop. "That's bad news, indeed. I loved my parents, even if they weren't my real mother and father."

"And they, from all accounts, loved you," Aramis assured him. "But that is all in the past. Right now, my young prince, it's time for you to make your decision."

"About staking my claim to the throne?" Philippe said.

"Precisely," Aramis answered. "But first, I must tell you something. Even if you refuse to challenge your brother, I won't return you to your dreadful cell in the Bastille. That would be too cruel a fate for one like you."

"You're very kind," said Philippe.

"I'm nothing of the sort," Aramis replied. "You're a prince, after all. And I'm a loyal Frenchman. Just say the word and I'll see that you get a home in the countryside. It would be like the farm where you grew up, except in a more secluded part of the world. So secluded, in fact, that none of your enemies will ever find you."

That sounded pretty good to Philippe. He pictured himself lying in the shade of a big, old tree, listening to bird songs and enjoying the scents of the great outdoors.

"You can do whatever tickles your fancy," Aramis continued. "And you need never hear about your brother or the royal court again."

Philippe looked at him. "Never?"

"Never," his companion promised. "You have my word on it."

Philippe shook his head. "There's got to be a catch."

"No catch," Aramis assured him. "No one will bother you. No one will ask anything of you. You can live out your days in peace and quiet."

Philippe considered the offer. The problem was, he didn't want to neglect his duty to the people of his kingdom. If Louis was as bad a ruler as Aramis said, France needed a new king right away.

But what if Louis *wasn't* so bad? What if Aramis had been exaggerating the problem? There was only one way for Philippe to know that for certain.

"I have a favor to ask," he told his companion.

"A favor?" Aramis echoed.

"Yes. I would like to see my brother in action—with my own eyes. Only then can I make a thoughtful decision."

Aramis nodded. "Your wisdom is kingly, indeed." His eyes narrowed. "Very well, then. You'll have a chance to see your brother in action—but only briefly. Then you must decide one way or the other."

Philippe promised that he would do that. Then, as the carriage swayed back and forth on its way out of the city of Paris, he laid his head on his paws, settled into the seat cushion, and dozed off.

Chapter Seven

Feeling a breeze caress his face, Wishbone opened one eye. But he wasn't in a wooden carriage, rumbling over the cobblestones of old Paris.

He was in Joe's bedroom, sleeping at the foot of his pal's bed. The breeze had come through a half-open window, where a full moon rode a dark sky full of silver clouds.

Wishbone got up on all four paws. Then he walked around the bed and took a look at Joe, who was illuminated by a patch of moonlight.

Joe was sleeping as contentedly as Wishbone had ever seen him, a smile pulling at the corners of his mouth. He was probably dreaming about playing catcher for the traveling team.

But Wishbone knew Joe wouldn't be dreaming those dreams for long. Sooner or later, he would find out how Damont had duped him, and he would feel awful—and not just because he hadn't made the team.

Of course, by then Damont would be class president and there would be nothing Joe or anyone else could do about it. The time to act was now, while there was still a chance of exposing Damont's scheme.

Wishbone hopped up and put his paws on the edge of Joe's bed. *But what can just one terrier do?* he thought.

He had asked himself the same kind of question all day long, over and over again. How could he open Joe's eyes to what was going on? How could he keep his pal from being made a fool of?

Suddenly, Wishbone got an idea. If he could snatch Joe's catcher's mask and hide it somewhere, Joe wouldn't be able to play catcher until Ted and the others got a new one. Maybe Ted would even become upset with Joe for losing the mask. Then he might show Joe his true colors.

Wishbone looked around Joe's room. He saw his friend's mitt sitting on his dresser, along with his bright red baseball cap and his crinkled, old batting gloves. Wishbone even spotted Joe's wooden bat, propped up against a wall in one corner of the room. But for the life of him, the terrier couldn't find Joe's mask.

"Where could the thing have gone?" he wondered.

He sniffed around for it. Normally, there was nothing more dependable than Wishbone's nose. He had a sense of smell that could pick out the delicate scent of a cookie at a hundred yards.

But even his sense of smell wasn't doing him any good when it came to locating the catcher's mask. He knew what it smelled like, but he couldn't catch even a whiff of it.

Wishbone jumped up the rest of the way onto Joe's bed and stood next to the boy's elbow, which was underneath his blanket. Joe stirred a little, but he didn't wake up.

"I'll look around from up here," Wishbone said. "Maybe I'll find a clue that'll lead me to the mask."

And look around he did. But it didn't seem to help. There was still no sign of the catcher's mask. He padded around Joe to another part of the bed. Still, he met with the same result.

In other words, none at all. As far as he could tell, the mask had disappeared into thin air.

"Well," Wishbone said, "this is getting me nowhere fast."

Not that he was getting discouraged. Not a great detective like him, no way. In fact, he was just getting warmed up.

Instead of using his nose to sniff out the mask, Wishbone decided to begin poking around for it in Joe's closet. If that approach didn't work, there were always Joe's dresser drawers.

"Eventually," Wishbone promised himself, "I'll find it. It's purely a matter of time."

Negotiating a path around the terrain of Joe's sleeping form, Wishbone made his way to the edge of the bed again. But as he did this, his foot brushed against something hard. It wasn't a knee or a foot or an elbow or any of the other lumps Wishbone had expected.

"Ah-ha!" he said, pushing the hard thing with his nose. "And what do we have here?"

Taking hold of the edge of the blanket with his teeth, Wishbone very carefully pulled it back. After all, he didn't want to wake up Joe if he could help it. Joe tried to reach for the blanket in his sleep, but Wishbone continued to peel it away.

After a couple of seconds, he began to see what it was he'd felt under the blankets. If he hadn't been afraid of waking Joe from his sleep, Wishbone would have howled with triumph.

"It's the mask!" he declared.

Sure enough, the thing was sitting there on the bedsheet, dark and mysterious. It was almost as if it had some magical fascination for Joe, some mystical power over him.

"I mean, sleeping with the contraption!" Wishbone exclaimed to himself. "Talk about taking things a little too far."

But now that Wishbone had dug up the mask, he could bury it somewhere for real. In the yard, maybe. Or, better yet, in the yard of their neighbor, Wanda.

Then, when Joe had come to his senses and given Damont a run for his money, Wishbone could dig up the mask again. "I don't want to keep it," he said. "I just want to make it go away for a while."

Hunkering down, he latched on to the mask with his teeth. It had a salty taste, like Wanda's pot roast. Getting a good grip, Wishbone began to pull it away from its special place at Joe's side.

But before he could move the mask more than a few inches, Joe's arm flopped over it and pinned it down. Wishbone tried to tug at the thing, but it wouldn't budge. Joe's arm was putting too much weight on the mask.

"Desperate times call for desperate measures," the terrier said. "Maybe if I tug on it a little harder . . ."

And that was what he did. Wishbone yanked on it twice as hard as before. Lo and behold, the catcher's mask started to slide over the bedsheet, despite the weight of Joe's arm.

"Now we're getting somewhere," Wishbone said. But no sooner had he begun to make progress than Joe's fingers hooked themselves into the frame of the mask. And though he still appeared to be asleep, Joe tugged the thing back to his chest.

Wishbone hauled it away again, moving it a few inches toward the edge of the bed. And again, the

sleeping kid pulled it back. Forward and back went the catcher's mask, forward and back like the prize in a tug-of-war.

"This is frustrating," the terrier said wearily, "not to mention more than a little exhausting."

He decided to gamble everything on one big tug. After all, faint heart never won fair lady . . . or an old baseball mask.

Shifting his jaw to improve his grasp on the mask, Wishbone braced his legs and wrenched at it for all he was worth. He was a lot stronger than he looked, too. After all, he ate only the best doggie treats and kept himself in tiptop shape.

As hard as Wishbone tugged on the catcher's mask, he just couldn't free it from Joe's iron grip. But he did accomplish one feat—the exact thing he'd been trying to avoid.

He woke Joe up.

The boy blinked in the darkness, trying to figure out what was happening. Looking down, he saw the mask in his hands. He also saw Wishbone's teeth clamped onto it.

"Wishbone!" he hissed. "What do you think you're doing?"

"Man," said the terrier, releasing the mask reluctantly and backing up a few steps. "It looks like the jig is up."

Joe eased himself down again onto his pillow, clutching the mask to him tighter than ever. He covered himself up again with his blanket. Then he began to doze off as if he'd never woken up at all.

In a matter of seconds, he had that smile on his face again. Wishbone snuffled and jumped down to the floor. It seemed he'd lost the battle for the mask—and for Joe's self-respect.

But I have only begun to fight, he thought.

It wouldn't be easy to get Joe to forget about that mask and run against Damont. But somehow, Wishbone would find a way. . . .

Chapter Eight

$\mathcal{T}$he weekend went by quickly. Suddenly, it was Monday.

Wishbone hadn't made any progress in getting Joe to see the truth about the traveling team. But he had decided to accompany his pal to school, figuring he would run into Red, Flip, and Lefty.

If he followed the older boys around, maybe they would lead him to something he could use to open Joe's eyes. Anyway, it was worth a try.

As always, Joe stopped at David's house to ring the bell. David and Joe walked to school together all the time, and today wasn't going to be an exception.

The boys talked about movies they had seen recently. They talked about sports. They even talked about homework.

But they didn't talk about the election for class president. It was as if David had decided not to bother Joe about it anymore.

After all, Joe had given David and Samantha his answer about running, and the answer had been "no."

Still, it couldn't have been easy for David to accept his friend's decision. Damont's campaign posters were pasted or nailed up everywhere.

They were stapled to trees as well as telephone poles. As if that weren't enough, Wishbone ran across a crumpled "Damont for President" leaflet every few feet.

Then he saw something that *really* got him hot under the dog collar. Damont had pasted a bumper sticker on Wishbone's favorite tree!

"Of all the nerve," he said, seething. "Somebody's got to do something about this kid. And it's got to be done *before* the town gets buried in an avalanche of campaign *litter*ature."

Then, as if on cue, a loud voice blared at them from a place they couldn't see—a place over a rise in the road, Wishbone thought. Even though the voice was distorted a little, Wishbone recognized it instantly.

It belonged to Damont. Who else?

"A vote for Damont Jones is a vote for progress!" the voice thundered. "Damont Jones—the future of Sequoyah Middle School!"

A moment later, a white station wagon came over the rise in the road. It had "Vote for Damont" signs hanging out its windows and an even bigger "Damont for President" sign strapped to its roof.

Damont's uncle was driving the car—and he was going much more slowly than he should have. There was a lineup of cars behind him, their drivers looking impatient at the delay.

Damont himself was sitting in the passenger's seat, booming out his campaign slogans with a big, silver bullhorn. Every time he passed a sixth-grader walking to school, he had his uncle come almost to a dead stop so he could hand out another leaflet.

"Don't forget to vote!" he told everyone he came across. "Most of all, don't forget to vote for *me!*"

David stopped in his tracks and rolled his eyes. "Tell me this isn't happening," he said.

Joe didn't answer his friend. He just looked at Damont's wild campaign antics and frowned.

He wasn't the only one, either. An elderly couple had stopped and was holding their hands over their ears.

"That young man has some nerve," said the woman.

"And a lack of consideration for other people," remarked the man.

"You can say that again," Wishbone added.

But the worst was yet to come. As Wishbone looked on, Damont signaled for his uncle to pull over to the side of the road—much to the relief of the drivers lined up behind him. Then the Damonster hopped out of the car and began handing something out.

At first, Wishbone thought they were more of the leaflets of which Damont was so fond. Then he realized they were too small to be leaflets.

"That's right!" Damont shouted. "Come and get your certificate for a free ice-cream sundae, compliments of Damont Jones—the candidate who cares!"

"Oh, no," said David. "Now he's *buying* votes."

It was true. Damont couldn't have gotten any more underhanded if he had tried. Still, it was pretty hard for kids to resist a free sundae.

In what seemed like only a second or two, a crowd of sixth-graders had gathered around Damont, making a circle two and three deep. Damont grinned, obviously pleased that his plan was working so well.

Of course, with a free sundae to lure them on, some of those sixth-graders had come from across the street—and more were still coming. The drivers who had been keeping up a turtle's pace behind Damont's uncle's car now had to stop altogether. Otherwise, they would have risked hitting one of the kids.

With the sidewalk blocked by the crowd, the elderly couple couldn't easily get by. They and everyone else—including students from other grades trying to get to school—had to walk onto the lawn of a nearby house to continue on their way.

Damont was trampling on everyone's rights. What was more upsetting was that he didn't care, as long as it suited his own selfish purposes.

After a moment or two, the lady who lived in the house where the lawn was being trampled came outside and made her way through the crowd. Wishbone recognized the woman as one of Ellen's co-workers at the town library.

"Excuse me," she said, directing her comments at

Damont. "This is a public nuisance, not to mention a safety hazard, young man. You ought to stop what you're doing immediately and let these children go to school."

Damont pretended to be hurt. "Ma'am," he said, "this is democracy in action. It's what made our country great. Would you put a halt to the great democratic process here in Oakdale?"

The woman hesitated for just a moment. And that, Wishbone told himself, was when Damont knew he had her.

"After all," the presidential candidate went on, raising his voice so everyone within earshot could hear him, "young people are the future. Aren't we?"

His question was met with a rousing cheer—and several more requests for free ice-cream certificates. The woman and her protest were all but forgotten.

Wishbone shook his head. "With a future like the one Damont's got planned, I'd rather live in the past."

He turned to look back at David and Joe. David had opened his mouth as if to say something to his friend. Then he must have thought better of it, because he remained silent.

Even so, Wishbone heard David loud and clear. "I still want Joe to run against Damont," he told David, "just like you do." He wagged his short, white tail. "But I can't ask him any more than you can."

Wishbone gazed at Joe. If the terrier knew his pal, Joe was just as upset with Damont as David and Wishbone were. Maybe, just for a moment, he had even been tempted to do something about it. But in the end, it seemed, his dream of being on the traveling baseball team still came first.

"C'mon," Joe told David. "Let's get out of here."

Making their way around the crowd that surrounded Damont, they resumed their walk to school. But it was a long time before the delighted echoes of Damont's new supporters faded in the distance.

As Wishbone padded along on the rough, hard sidewalk, it occurred to him that Damont was a lot like King Louis, Philippe's brother. Of course, Philippe didn't know that right away. He had to see it with his own eyes.

Chapter Nine

Again, Wishbone imagined that he was Philippe. But he was no longer a prisoner, thanks to Aramis. Now he was in the woods near an estate called Vaux, where a big party was being held for King Louis.

They had traveled all night to reach this place. However, Aramis had said it was important to do so. After all, Philippe had asked to see his brother in action—and it was in Vaux that he would see it.

As Philippe got out of the carriage that had rescued him from prison, he felt the soft, mossy ground under his paws. He listened to the sound of gurgling waters from a distant stream and heard the chittering of unseen creatures. He inhaled the perfumed forest air and enjoyed the caress of the warm summer breezes.

Philippe wagged his tail with delight. Eight years in a prison cell had made him forget such simple pleasures. He was glad for the chance to experience them again.

Aramis followed Philippe out of the carriage. "Come," he said. "It's almost time for breakfast."

"Breakfast?" Philippe wondered.

His stomach growled, reminding him how empty

it was. Maybe he could find a scrap or two to eat when no one was looking.

Together, Philippe and Aramis left their driver behind and headed for the fringe of the forest, where it opened onto a great green lawn. There were tables and chairs set up everywhere. In a shaded spot nearby, a couple of very long tables groaned under the weight of meats and cheeses and fruits and luscious-looking pastries.

"Everything smells wonderful," said Philippe. "No, *better* than wonderful."

Aramis put out a hand, keeping Philippe from going any farther. "We'll stop here," he advised, his voice a whisper. "That way, we'll be able to see and hear all that goes on, without being spotted ourselves."

Philippe agreed that that was a good idea. He hunkered down behind a bush and waited with Aramis. They didn't have to wait very long for something to happen. Soon, a procession of finely dressed lords and ladies came walking in their direction from behind a long, rolling hill.

"Wow!" said Philippe, keeping his voice down to a whisper, too.

He had never seen so many rich people in one place. In fact, he had hardly ever seen any rich people at all.

There were guards in evidence, as well. Musketeers, in fact. But they stayed in the background as the lords and ladies came closer to Philippe.

Aramis pointed to a figure dressed in a wig and a gold-colored waistcoat. "See that one? At the head of the procession?"

Philippe squinted. After all, the sun was rising behind the man, making it difficult to see his face clearly.

"I think so," Philippe replied.

"Keep an eye on him," Aramis told him.

Philippe did his best to do what Aramis suggested. At first, he didn't understand why. Then the man moved out of line with the sun and his features became easier to make out. Philippe recognized the fur, the markings. Then he leaped back a step and landed on all four feet.

"It's . . . it's me!" he said, his voice an excited whisper. "I mean . . . it's him! My brother!"

Indeed, it was King Louis. It was one thing to see his face on a coin—but quite another to see him in person. Louis was much more dignified-looking than Philippe had expected.

Dignified . . . but also sort of snooty.

"See to my mother," Louis told a tall, slender man at his side. "The old biddy will want her favorite pastries set aside for her. Not that she needs them, since she has become so fat."

"As you wish, sire," said the man.

"Fat?" Philippe echoed. "That's not a very nice way to describe one's mother."

"Louis is not a very nice fellow," Aramis explained. "But hush, my friend . . . he's not finished with his instructions."

"Oh," the king went on, "and make sure our host, Fouquet, knows how much I like to win at cards. I won't be very happy at evening's end without a large pile of gold coins in front of me."

"Whatever you desire, my lord," the man replied.

"My brother cheats at cards?" Philippe asked Aramis.

"Worse than that," the bearded man replied. "He makes others cheat *for* him. But the result is the same."

"And one other thing," Louis told the man. "I have heard it said that the fireworks tonight will be breathtaking. If they are anything less, I will be disappointed—and when I am disappointed, people suffer."

The man nodded obediently. "I will inform our host, my king."

Finally, bowing low, the man backed away from Louis. A moment later, he was gone.

"The men who make the fireworks are hard workers," Aramis said. "But it's difficult to impress the king. And, as you heard him say, he'll take his disappointment out on everyone."

Just then, the king's mother appeared. As elegantly as she was dressed, she couldn't have been anyone else. Philippe looked at her carefully. She was older than the woman he remembered visiting him as a child, and she had a beauty mark on her cheek.

"It's the same woman," Aramis whispered to him, as if he could read what was on Philippe's mind. "The beauty mark's not real. It's something she paints on these days."

"She's still beautiful," Philippe observed. "And she's not very fat at all, despite what my brother said."

Louis bowed as he took note of his mother's presence. "My dear lady," he said, "you are as radiant as ever."

Philippe snorted. "That's not what he said a moment ago."

"The king has become very good at lying," Aramis told him. "In fact, it's one of his most impressive talents."

"You are too kind," the king's mother told Louis.

"So I've heard it said," the king replied.

His mother frowned ever so slightly. Then she curtsied and withdrew from the king's presence.

"She didn't seem happy with him," Philippe observed.

Aramis turned to him. "Would *you* be happy if Louis were *your* son?"

Philippe saw someone else walking over to speak with his brother.

"Look," he said. "Here comes somebody."

This man was short and round, with rosy cheeks that looked like apples. "Your pardon, sire," he said. "Will you be sitting for your portrait this afternoon, as we discussed?"

Louis stopped and looked at him. "My dear fellow," he said, placing his hands on the man's shoulders, "of course I'll be sitting for my portrait. I can think of nothing more important than bringing beauty to the world—and what could be more beautiful than another painting of *me?*"

The man smiled. "Of course, sire. And the bill . . . ?"

"It will be paid immediately, as always," the king assured him. "Put down whatever figure you like, my friend. After all, how can one place a price on the likeness of a king?"

The man's smile widened. "It will be done, sire." Then, just as the first man had done, he bowed low and then backed away.

"Well," said Philippe, "at least he's not a cheapskate."

"Not when it comes to showering gifts on himself," Aramis replied.

A third man approached. This one was as thin as the first man and as short as the second. His chin was pointy and he wore a moustache that was curled up at its ends.

"Sire," he said, "the new waistcoat you ordered—"

Louis glared at him. He was angry all of a sudden. "Don't tell me it isn't ready. I've already agreed to sit for my portrait this afternoon."

The man held his hands up. "Oh, it's ready," he said. "It's just that the materials that went into making it had to be obtained at great cost. As a result, the bill will be a trifle higher than I intended."

Louis dismissed the problem with a flip of his hand. "Don't trouble me with such small concerns. When have I ever objected to paying a little more for an item of superior quality?"

"Never," said the man. "But then, you are a most generous monarch." Like the others, he bowed and retreated.

"Yes," said Louis, if only to himself. "I *am* a most generous monarch. In fact, I may be the most generous monarch Europe has ever known."

"That's certainly the truth," Aramis commented drily.

Louis was approached by yet another man. This one was tall and broad and powerful-looking, with a silver-gray moustache. He wasn't dressed the way the others were. He wore the blue waistcoat and silver sash of a high-ranking soldier—a general, perhaps.

"I beg your pardon," the man told the king, "but I need your help in a most serious matter, sire."

Louis eyed him a bit suspiciously. "And what is that?" he asked.

The man frowned. "Your soldiers and their families are starving, Your Majesty. Time and again, they have risked their lives to defend your kingdom—yet they haven't been paid in months. If you could pay them only a small fraction of what you owe them—"

"See here," said Louis, cutting off the man's remarks. The king's eyes blazed with anger. "Do I look to you as if I'm made of money? France's soldiers will be paid in good time. In the meantime, they should be happy with what they've got—which is a lot more than some people have."

The man sighed. "Sire, I beg of you—"

Suddenly, Louis drew his paw back and slapped the man across the face.

"That's enough," he said. "I won't have the leader of my own army bothering me while I'm having breakfast."

The general hesitated a moment. Then he spoke again. "Still, Your Majesty, I must protest. My soldiers—"

The king hit the man a second time. And a third.

By then, the man's face was red on both sides. But he persisted. "Sire, you may cause me pain, but it's nothing compared to what my men must endure. If only—"

"Silence!" Louis raged at the top of his voice.

His face was a dangerous shade of red, and his eyes were so big that Philippe thought they would pop out of his head.

Louis pointed a paw at the general's face. It shook with his royal anger.

"I warned you!" he rasped.

Then he gestured for a couple of his guards to come over. When the musketeers reached the king, Louis dismissed the general with a wave of his hand.

"Have this man sent to the Bastille," he commanded.

"As you wish," said one of the musketeers, though he paled at the idea.

The general didn't say anything more. He just lifted his chin and allowed the musketeers to escort him away.

"You see?" asked Aramis. "And this is the man

who rules our beloved France. He is generous indeed when it comes to himself. But when the truly needy ask for his help . . ."

". . . he turns them down," said Philippe.

"And, if it suits him, he also punishes them horribly," Aramis added.

Philippe nodded. "Yes, my friend, I see that quite clearly."

He gazed a while longer at his brother. Clearly, everything Aramis had told Philippe about Louis was true. Philippe had seen and heard it for himself. And it had been chilling to see someone with Philippe's own face and brown spots acting in such a mean-spirited way.

Louis was trampling cruelly on the rights of his people. He was draining the treasury to suit his own expensive tastes. In short, he didn't deserve to be king. Unless he was stopped, France and all her citizens would be ruined.

Philippe couldn't let that happen. He *wouldn't* let that happen.

He turned to Aramis. "The thought of a safe, secure life is a tempting one," he said. "But I don't want to live in the country and chase squirrels. I want to replace my brother, Louis, on the throne. I want to bring justice to the people of France."

Aramis looked at him seriously. "Are you sure about this?"

Philippe nodded. "I'm *very* sure."

"Good," said Aramis. He handed Philippe a folded piece of paper. "Then read this carefully, my friend. Your life may depend on it."

Chapter Ten

Wishbone heard a squeal and jumped. It had sounded to him like car tires skidding over an asphalt road.

But how could that be? There weren't any cars in seventeenth-century France. There were only horse-drawn carriages, and the one that had taken him to Vaux was hidden safely back in the woods.

Then Wishbone realized he wasn't *in* seventeenth-century France. He was in twentieth-century Oakdale. Raising his head, he saw where the squealing was coming from.

"I might have known," he said to himself.

One of Damont's campaign banners had dropped into the street and was tying up auto traffic in the intersection near Sequoyah Middle School. One end was still nailed to a tree on one side of the street, but the other end had come loose.

As a result, the cars on all four sides of the intersection had come to a halt. The drivers weren't too happy about the situation, either.

One of them got out of his car and tore down the

banner, then read it aloud. "'Damont Doesn't Just Promise. He Delivers.'"

Frowning, the driver balled up the banner and stuffed it under his arm. Then he took it back to his car with him.

"There oughtta be a law against nailing banners up," Wishbone growled. "In fact, there probably *is* a law. Damont has just decided to ignore it in the name of democracy."

The terrier got to his feet. It seemed that he had dozed off in the sun-warmed grass alongside the school building.

Wishbone looked around. Judging by the height of the sun in the sky, the kids would be getting out of school in an hour or so. He would have to be alert, so he could track Red and his friends and maybe find a way to lead Joe to the truth.

Suddenly, the terrier heard a smack. It had come from around the corner, where the school's ball fields were located. Curious, he followed the sound to its source.

He saw three people in the schoolyard. One was an adult in a bright red sweater, who was standing with his back to Wishbone. The other two were boys maybe a little older than Joe.

One of the boys was crouching behind home plate in catcher's gear. The other one was standing on the pitcher's mound, holding a baseball behind his back. As Wishbone watched, the boy on the mound went into his windup and threw a sizzling fastball. The catcher snagged it in his glove.

"'Atta boy!" cried the adult, as the kid in the catcher's gear threw the ball back. "Keep it up, Dan!"

Wishbone couldn't see the adult's face, so he

found a hole in the fence near the ground and poked his head through. With a better view, everything fell into place.

The adult was Mr. Bernardi, one of the gym teachers at Joe's school. If memory served—and a great detective's memory never failed him—Mr. Bernardi also happened to be the coach of the seventh-grade traveling team. The man had a big, black handlebar moustache.

Obviously, the boys on the mound and behind the plate had a free period now. If a kid was on a school team, it wasn't unusual to spend a free period with his or her coach.

The boy on the mound wound up again and threw the baseball as hard as before. Again, the coach cheered and the catcher tossed the ball back.

After a few more throws, Mr. Bernardi told the kids to hold up. Then he walked out to the mound. The boy in catcher's gear walked out there, too.

"You're doing great," the coach told his pitcher. "Just remember to bend your back and follow through, and you'll be fine."

The boy smiled. "Thanks, Coach."

Then Mr. Bernardi turned to his catcher. "You're giving him a great target, Bobby. Keep it up. But don't forget to keep your throwing hand behind your back, so it doesn't get hurt."

The kid nodded. "I'll try, Coach."

At that moment, another adult walked out onto the field. Wishbone recognized him as Mr. Hooton, a lawyer in town. Mr. Hooton's son Danny was a sixth-grader, just like Joe.

"Coach Bernardi?" he called.

The coach didn't seem all that eager to greet

Mr. Hooton. Still, he walked up to him and shook his hand.

"You know, we don't really encourage parents to walk around the school grounds," said the coach. "That is, unless you have an appointment to speak with someone."

"I'm too busy to make appointments," Mr. Hooton told him. "Now, about this traveling team of yours. As I told you last spring, my boy Danny would make a terrific shortstop on that team. He's quick, he's got good hands, and he's got an excellent arm." The man held his hands out. "But Danny and I haven't received a single call about tryouts. I hope you're not going to tell me you've decided to overlook him."

Coach Bernardi sighed. "Mr. Hooton, Danny is a sixth-grader."

"So?" said Mr. Hooton.

"So we're no longer allowed to carry sixth-graders on our team. Believe me, I wanted to bring up some new players the way we have in the past. We've been very successful in doing that. But the rules have changed."

"Can't we have them changed back?" asked Mr. Hooton. "It doesn't seem fair."

Mr. Bernardi shrugged. "It's the same for every team, all over the state. I can't get the rules changed all by myself. I've got to live with them, like everyone else."

Mr. Hooton wasn't happy about that state of affairs. But Wishbone had stopped following the conversation. He was more interested in what he had already learned.

"No longer allowed to carry sixth-graders on the

traveling team," he echoed. His tail wagged. "Now, just a minute. If only seventh-graders can play, and Joe's a sixth-grader . . . he's obviously wasting his time. He can't make the team no matter *how* hard he practices."

But that wasn't bad news. Wishbone had suspected Joe was being bamboozled all along, one way or the other. In fact, this was good news . . .

. . . because he had finally found a way to expose Damont's underhanded scheme!

Wishbone remained on the grounds of the school, pacing back and forth, for what seemed like a very long time. His tail wagged with anticipation.

After all, what he had in mind was pretty big—and pretty bold.

If he was going to help his pal Joe, he would have to go where few dogs had gone before: school. He just hoped he didn't get kicked out before he could carry out his plan.

Finally, three o'clock arrived. Classes were over. As the students started to spill out of the school's main entrance, Wishbone darted past them straight into the building.

Wishbone didn't know where Joe's classroom was. But he had his trusty sense of smell with which to track the boy down.

Of course, there were lots of other smells in the school. Each kid had his own scent; on top of that, someone had been baking cookies. Wishbone took a whiff. Oatmeal, too—his favorite.

But he couldn't think about cookies now. Wishbone

was on a mission. Concentrating on Joe's particular scent, he wove his way through a forest of legs.

He couldn't help but notice all the colorful drawings on the walls, or the open doors that allowed him to glimpse classroom after classroom. He even saw a room where every wall was full of books.

Wishbone wished that someday he would have the chance to explore the school building at his leisure. Darting through it this way was very frustrating. He wanted to see and smell everything, but there just wasn't time.

Little by little, Joe's scent got stronger. Wishbone continued to zig and zag his way through the hall, drawing giggles and exclamations of surprise from the kids.

Finally, he caught sight of Joe. He was walking down the hall by himself, deep in thought—probably dreaming about his next traveling team practice, if Wishbone knew his pal.

Suddenly, Joe saw him. The boy's mouth fell open. "Wishbone!" he said. "What are you doing here?"

"Just trying to open your eyes," Wishbone told him.

With that, he clamped his teeth on the bottom of his pal's pants leg. Then he began to tug for all he was worth.

"Hey!" said Joe. "What's gotten into you?"

Coach Bernardi's office was just down the hall and to the right. Wishbone tried to pull Joe in that direction.

Unfortunately, Joe was too big to be pulled. "Okay," said Wishbone. "Time for Plan B."

With that, he homed in on a different scent—that

of Coach Bernardi. After all, he'd picked up on the coach's smell earlier that day—and once Wishbone filed a scent away in his sensory memory bank, he never forgot it.

Down the hall, around a corner to the right—and there it was. The coach's office.

Joe was following right behind Wishbone. After all, the last thing the boy would want was to see his dog run amok in school.

"Wishbone," Joe called from behind. "You've got to cut this out. Wishbone!"

But the terrier wasn't about to stop at that point. Not when his objective was so close he could smell it. And that wasn't just an expression. He really *could* smell the coach's office and everything in it, from the man's cologne to a half-eaten tuna fish sandwich.

As luck would have it, the door to Coach Bernardi's office was wide open. Without a second thought, Wishbone dashed inside and leaped up onto a chair.

Grabbing the door jamb, Joe swung into the office, too.

The coach looked up from his desk, where he was signing some papers. He eyed Joe, then Wishbone, then Joe again.

"Well," Coach Bernardi said, "this is something you don't see every day. Is there anything that I can do for you, son?"

Joe blushed. "Actually, sir, I didn't mean to barge in." He glanced at Wishbone. "My dog sort of . . ." He shrugged.

Coach Bernardi smiled at Wishbone, then at Joe. "I understand, son. I used to have a dog like that myself." He leaned back in his chair. "But I've got a

94

busy afternoon ahead of me, so maybe we can chat later."

Joe nodded. "Okay." He picked Wishbone up and left Coach Bernardi's office as quickly as he could, more than a little embarrassed.

Wishbone's heart sank. After all the trouble he'd gone to in order to bring Joe face to face with Coach Bernardi, he couldn't let his friend leave without learning the truth.

Pulling free of Joe's grasp, Wishbone landed on all fours. He skidded a little on the slippery school floor, then ran back into the coach's office.

"Wishbone!" Joe hissed, exasperated.

Once again, Wishbone jumped up on the chair in the coach's office. Once again, Joe was forced to come in after him.

Coach Bernardi looked up and smiled at them again. "I know I said we could talk later, but this is a bit sooner than I had in mind."

"Me, too," Joe replied, blushing even redder than before.

"Introduce yourself," Wishbone told Joe. "Go ahead, Joe. I'm telling you, this is your chance."

The boy must have been thinking the same thing, because he said, "Er . . . my name's Joe—Joe Talbot." He pointed to the terrier. "And this is Wishbone."

Coach Bernardi nodded. "I know who you are, Joe. I've seen you play ball." He eyed Wishbone. "And now that I think about it, I've seen your dog, too."

"It's nice to be noticed," Wishbone said.

"It's nice to see you," said Coach Bernardi. "Both of you. But I really *do* have a lot of work to do."

"Don't worry," Joe told the coach. "We won't bother you again, sir." He threw a cautionary look in Wishbone's direction. "I'll make sure of it."

Wishbone lowered his head. He'd tried as hard as he could, but this wasn't working the way he'd thought it would. Unfortunately, he would have to find some other way to open Joe's eyes.

"Too bad," he said. "This seemed like such a good plan at the time."

Joe started out into the hall. But just before he closed the door behind him, he turned to look at the coach again. The boy cleared his throat.

Coach Bernardi looked at him. He wasn't smiling anymore. "Is there something else, son?"

"I just thought I'd tell you," Joe replied, "we might be seeing a lot of each other. I'm trying out to be your new catcher—on the seventh-grade traveling team, I mean."

The coach tilted his head, obviously more than a little surprised. "You're trying out?" he echoed.

Joe shrugged. "I know I'm just a sixth-grader, but

I've been working out with Red and some of the other guys. They told me I had a real good shot at getting the job." He shrugged again. "Red said I've got a cannon for an arm, and I might throw out a runner or two."

Coach Bernardi's expression became a lot more serious all of a sudden. "Red said that?"

Joe looked as if he was starting to realize something was wrong. "Uh-huh. Flip and Lefty said so, too."

The coach frowned. "They shouldn't have told you that, Joe. I've already got a catcher in mind for the team. Besides, the league rules have changed. We're not allowed to carry any sixth-graders this year."

Joe swallowed hard. "You're not?" he asked in a small voice. "But Red and the other guys—"

"They were leading you on," Coach Bernardi explained. "But for the life of me, I can't imagine why they would do such a thing. They knew about the rule change, and they're good friends with the boy I picked to be catcher."

The coach stroked his chin for a moment, then got to his feet.

"Stay right here, Joe," he said. "I'm going to have to look into this. I don't know what's going on, but I'll make it my business to find out."

In a matter of minutes, the coach had found Red, Flip, and Lefty, and brought them into his office. It was getting a little crowded in there, but Wishbone didn't care. Like any great detective, he would have endured much worse to get to the truth of the situation.

Coach Bernardi sat down and eyed Red from the other side of his desk. "So," he said, "Joe, here, tells me he's been attending practices with you guys. Is that true?"

Red wouldn't look at the coach. He just stared at the floor and shuffled his feet.

"A sure sign of guilt," Wishbone told himself.

"Well," Red replied at last, "he's been working out with us."

"Just working out?" Coach Bernardi prodded. "Or did you tell Joe he was participating in official team practices?"

Red shrugged. "Practices, I guess."

The coach nodded. "I see. And did you tell Joe he had a shot at making the team? Being our catcher?"

Red took a deep breath, then let it out. "I . . . uh . . . might have told him that." He glanced at his friends. "Or maybe it was Flip."

"It was *you*," Flip said quickly.

"But all of you gave Joe that impression," said the coach. "No one told him he wasn't allowed to play on the team, or that he didn't have a prayer of playing catcher for us, no matter how good he was. Is that right?"

No one spoke for a moment or two. Then Red said, "Right."

Coach Bernardi shook his head. "I don't get it, guys. Why would you do a thing like that? Just to be mean?" He thought for a moment. "No," he decided, "there's got to be more to it than that."

"Tell him about the money," Wishbone thought.

"It was Damont's idea," Lefty blurted out.

"Yeah," Flip admitted. "Damont."

"Who's that?" asked the coach.

The seventh-graders looked at one another. Finally, it was Red who provided Coach Bernardi with an explanation.

"Damont's another sixth-grader," the boy explained. "He's running for class president unopposed so far, and he was afraid that Joe might run against him. So he asked us to keep Joe busy." He shrugged. "You know, with practices and stuff. Damont said Joe wouldn't worry about running for president if he thought he was going to play on the traveling team."

"He paid us some money," Lefty said sheepishly. "Five dollars each, if we'd play along with his plan."

"Ah-ha!" said Wishbone. "The truth comes out at last!"

The coach studied Red, then Flip, then Lefty. The boys seemed to be pretty ashamed of themselves.

"You know what you did was wrong," said Coach Bernardi.

Red nodded. "I guess." He glanced at Joe. "Sorry."

"Yeah," Lefty echoed. "Nothing personal."

Joe didn't say anything. Obviously, he was too embarrassed. And shocked. And, of course, disappointed.

"I'm sorry, too," the coach told Joe. "I wish I could make it up to you somehow. As it is, I can only invite you to try out for the traveling team next year—for real."

Joe nodded. "I'll do that. For sure."

Coach Bernardi turned to Red and his friends. "I know you're sorry about what you did. In the future, you might want to think twice before pulling a bonehead play like this one. As it is, I'm going to suspend all three of you for the first three games of the season."

Wishbone could tell from the boys' expressions that the punishment wasn't an easy one to take. Still, none of them complained about it.

Last of all, the coach turned to Wishbone. "And as for you," he said, "you're welcome in my office anytime. If not for you, I would have never spoken to Joe, and we would never have gotten to the bottom of this."

"Thanks," said the terrier. "It's always gratifying to meet someone who appreciates your work."

Coach Bernardi sighed. "I just wish I could suspend Damont, as well. Unfortunately, he's not on the team, so there's not much I can do." He folded his arms across his chest. "The worst part is that he'll win the election if no one runs against him. Imagine someone with his sense of right and wrong serving as sixth-grade class president."

Wishbone nudged Joe's leg. "Yeah," he said, "imagine that."

Joe looked at the coach, then at Wishbone, then at the coach again. "Well," he said, "maybe Damont won't run unopposed, after all."

Chapter Eleven

Philippe and Aramis weren't able to eat a fancy breakfast like the one the king and his guests had laid out for them. They weren't able to eat a fancy lunch, either.

Still, the basket full of bread and fruit and wine that Aramis had packed seemed like a feast to Philippe. After all, he had been living on far worse fare in prison.

As they ate, Aramis introduced Philippe to their driver—a large, jolly man named Porthos. At the mention of the name, Philippe's eyes opened wide. He lifted his paw to shake Porthos's hand.

"You were a musketeer, too," he said.

"I see my fame has preceded me," said the big man.

"Along with your belly," Aramis joked.

Porthos glared at his friend, but only for a moment. Then he laughed.

"There are only three men on earth who can mock the great Porthos and not find themselves at the point of a sword. Fortunately for you, my friend Aramis, you are one of them."

Aramis nodded. "It is fortunate, indeed. But for which of us, I cannot say."

Porthos laughed again and clapped his old friend on the back. "I miss the old days, Aramis—the days of 'All for one and one for all!' Back then we were known far and wide for our courage and our skill with the sword."

Aramis smiled a bit as he remembered. "Yes," he said. "I miss those days, too."

Porthos winked at Philippe. "We used our flashing blades to defeat evil, power-hungry men and rescue lovely ladies, all in the name of the king . . . and, of course, the queen."

"But that was a different time," Aramis noted, reverting to his usual, serious look. "And, I might add, a different king. And since we're no longer as young as we used to be, we have to use our wits instead of our swords these days."

Philippe's head filled with wonder. "I'm honored to be dining with such famous men. You will have to tell me about your adventures."

"There will be time enough for that later," Aramis told him. "Right now, I would prefer to discuss the list I gave you."

Philippe took the piece of paper out of his sleeve. "I have it right here," he said.

"Have you any questions?" Aramis asked.

"None," said Philippe.

"How much more time will you need to study it?" Porthos inquired.

"No time at all," Philippe assured him.

Aramis frowned. "Pardon my doubts, my friend, but I must remind you of how long you have been a

prisoner. That kind of existence serves to dull the memory a bit."

"The truth," said Philippe, "is that there is no better place to *sharpen* one's memory. I mean, it's not as if there are a great many other things to do there besides thinking and remembering. We didn't get Ping-Pong privileges, you know."

The older man grunted at the jest. "I was only suggesting that if you're uncertain on a few points, we can delay the execution of our plan another day or so . . . look for another opportunity, perhaps . . ."

"I'm not the *least* bit uncertain," Philippe told his benefactor. "Go ahead, test me if you're skeptical. I'll repeat everything like a scholar reciting his lesson to his teacher."

Aramis looked at him. "Very well, then," he said at last. "We'll begin with your family history."

Philippe snuffled. "My mother is Anne of Austria—the very regal-looking lady with silver hair whom we saw this morning. She has a big beauty mark on her cheek, though it's not real."

Aramis chuckled drily. "You seem to know *her* well enough. But what about your younger brother, the prince?"

Philippe thought for a moment. "You mean the Duc d'Orléans. He's a dark-haired man with a pale face. His wife is named Henrietta. She's pretty, with blond hair and green eyes. And she has a soft spot for the king."

"Very good," said Aramis. "And your advisors? Do you know them as well as you know your relatives?"

"As well as I know myself," Philippe replied confidently. "Monsieur Fouquet is the man who owns this splendid estate. He's tall and slender, with curly brown hair and a likable smile. He's also my minister of finance, the guy I rely on to run France's treasury."

"And who is just below him in the administration of finances?" Aramis asked.

"That would be Monsieur Colbert," Philippe told him. "Colbert is a rather ugly man with a large head, dark brows, and a very unpleasant disposition." He leaned a little closer to his companion. "I think he needs more roughage in his diet."

Aramis smiled. "Well done, Your Majesty. You've got a bright future ahead of you."

"Only with your help," Philippe told him. "Even with all the studying I've done, I can see myself being dogged by a number of problems. There's no way I'll be able to deal with them on my own."

"Don't worry," said Aramis. "I haven't gone to all this trouble just to abandon you at the moment you're likely to need me most. I'll be there at your side all the time—so often, in fact, you'll probably get sick of me."

Philippe shook his head and wagged his tail politely. "Get sick of the man who freed me from my captivity? Who took a lowly prisoner and put him on the throne of France? I don't think so, my friend."

Aramis nodded. "Just one more thing. You still have a very suspicious pair of eyes to deal with."

"I know who you mean," said Philippe. After all, he really *had* studied Aramis's letter. "D'Artagnan, the captain of the king's guards. A very dangerous fellow, or so you indicated. He has dark, wavy hair, and even darker, piercing eyes."

"Yes," said the older man. "A dangerous fellow, indeed, and one who has been a good friend to me over the years. In fact, Porthos and I fought at his side when we served as the king's musketeers."

"And was he as great a hero as you were?" Philippe asked.

"Greater," Porthos chimed in. "D'Artagnan was the best of us."

"The man has the sight of a hawk," Aramis commented. "And he's absolutely loyal to King Louis, despite your brother's faults. If anyone can see through our plot, D'Artagnan can."

Philippe swallowed. "And what if he does?"

"You will be hanged for your treachery," Aramis said. "And I will be hanged alongside you, though D'Artagnan will be sad to see me perish."

"I'll be careful to watch out for him," Philippe promised.

But he felt a chill at the thought of D'Artagnan. He didn't look forward to the time when he would have to meet the man face to face and convince him that Louis was still on the throne.

Chapter Twelve

It was late at night and Philippe was sniffing the scent of wild geese when he felt Aramis jostle him. He turned and looked up into the bearded man's face.

"It's time to put our plan into action," said Aramis.

With that, he jumped up into the carriage that had carried them to Vaux. Philippe leaped in after him, and Porthos shut the door. Then the big man climbed up into the driver's seat and got the horses moving. The carriage rumbled forward.

Philippe stuck his head out the window and gazed at the full moon. It watched them from a nest of clouds like a big, silver eye. Owls hooted in the woods around them. Philippe felt his heart pounding against his ribs and chills running up and down his spine.

This was it—the moment they had been waiting for. But would they succeed and place Philippe on the throne? Or would they fail and be hanged as traitors to the king?

Only time would tell.

Philippe and Aramis rode in silence for a while.

After all, the bearded man had said all he could say. The rest was up to Philippe.

Finally, Aramis stuck his head out of the carriage and spoke to his muscular friend. "I believe this is the spot, Porthos."

Philippe stuck his head out of the carriage's other window. He couldn't see anything unusual about the area. To him, it looked like any other place along the road—dark, and thick with green forest. It even smelled the same as any other place, sweet with summer scents.

But Porthos replied, "I believe you're right, Aramis." He reined in the horses with his great strength. Then he climbed down from his seat and opened the door for the others.

Aramis turned to Philippe. "This is where we get out."

"If you say so," Philippe replied. Before, he had felt prepared for this venture. Now, he was feeling a bit uncertain.

Philippe hopped down from the carriage, landing on his front paws. Then he watched Aramis step out. Porthos led the horses as they pulled the carriage behind some trees, concealing it. Then he tied the beasts to the branches of a big old oak tree.

From that point on, Aramis led the way. However, Philippe, for the life of him, couldn't see where the man was leading them. After a while, they stopped in front of a steep, overgrown hillside.

Aramis reached through some vines and closed his fingers around something underneath them. Then he pulled and opened a heavy, wooden door. Beyond it was a passage of some kind. It wasn't an earthen tunnel, but one with a wooden floor and walls and ceiling.

It was built as well as the farmhouse in which Philippe had grown up.

They went inside. Then Porthos closed the door behind them.

Just inside the doorway, a small, dark leather bag awaited them. It indicated to Philippe that one of the men had come this way before—and recently. Kneeling beside the bag, Aramis opened it and removed its contents.

A little oil lamp. A handful of wooden matches for lighting it. A handkerchief and two vials of some milky-looking substance. And finally, a set of three black masks—one for each of them.

With practiced ease, Aramis stood and lit the oil lamp. It cast a yellow glow on them, throwing monstrous shadows against the walls of the passageway. Then, still holding the lamp, he handed out the masks.

Porthos slipped Philippe's on over his head. "There you go," he said. "I mean, there you go, *Your Majesty.*"

"Thanks," Philippe gulped.

He didn't like the idea of wearing a mask anymore, iron or otherwise. Still, if it was absolutely necessary to put it on to accomplish their goal, he would do it.

Philippe turned to Aramis. "How do I look?"

Aramis smiled. "You'll look better in a crown."

Porthos picked up the handkerchief and the two vials. Then he opened one vial and poured a bit of its contents into the handkerchief. Philippe sniffed, but he couldn't smell much—just a hint of sweetness, like a meadow flower.

He recognized the scent, too. After all, he had a good memory for such things. It was the same aroma Philippe had smelled when he was kidnapped from his parents' farm years ago.

When Porthos was done, he stuffed the vials into his belt. But he kept the handkerchief in his oversized hand.

"Ready," he told Aramis.

Satisfied, his friend advanced along the length of the passage, casting the light of the lamp in front of him. Philippe followed directly behind him. Porthos brought up the rear.

At last, they came to a dead end—a wooden wall with a small panel set into it. Aramis glanced at Philippe, then at Porthos.

"This is it," he said. "Beyond this panel lies what everyone calls the Chamber of Morpheus, where our esteemed King Louis sleeps the sleep of the unsuspecting—if not the just. Let's try not to wake him."

Philippe felt his heart pounding even harder than before. This was it. Up until now, the whole plan had seemed like a dream. But now it was really happening. He screwed up his nerve and prepared himself for what lay ahead.

However, Aramis didn't open the panel—at least, not right away. Instead, he turned to Philippe. "Forgive me, Your Majesty," he said, "but I have to ask one more time."

Philippe looked at him. "Ask what?"

"Whether you wouldn't be happier watching birds in the country," the other man explained. "It won't be an easy life, you know, pretending to be someone else, always on your guard against someone figuring out your true identity. If you have any doubts, this is your last chance to consider them."

Philippe took a deep breath, then looked back the way they had come. At the far end of the passage, he could make out the outline of the door. If he turned around now, things would be a lot simpler. He could relax, do whatever he wanted, live out his life in peace and quiet.

But France would suffer, more and more every year, at the hands of a king who didn't care about the welfare of his people. Their once-glorious nation would become a bedraggled prisoner of Louis's wastefulness, just as Philippe had been a prisoner of the Bastille.

It hurt him even to think of it. He looked at Aramis.

"I didn't come this far to turn back now," he said.

The older man smiled and scratched Philippe affectionately behind his ears. "I'm glad to hear you say that, Your Majesty. I see that your father, the king, had at least *one* son who inherited his better qualities."

With that, he pushed ever so slightly on the panel in front of him. As if by magic, it swung open, revealing the Chamber of Morpheus. As Philippe followed Aramis inside, the appearance of the room took his breath away.

It had to have been the largest and most handsome room in the entire palace. Delicately painted golden vines flowed along all four walls, and each one ended in a flourish of pink or blue flowers. The wood of the washstand and the bed were carved of some fine, cherry-dark wood Philippe couldn't even name. The linens and the bedcoverings were made of the most luxurious silk.

The ceiling featured a painting of rosy-cheeked Morpheus, the Roman god of dreams, blowing a double handful of poppy flowers at anyone who chanced to look up at him.

"Er . . . nice place," Philippe murmured.

But the most astonishing thing about the room was not the way it was decorated. It was the figure who lay asleep in the middle of the chamber in an oversize, fluffy bed, his head resting comfortably on his paws. . . .

A figure that looked *exactly* like Philippe!

The former prisoner stood there, unable to move for a moment. Looking at Louis was like looking in a mirror. It didn't seem real. And yet, there he was.

But the king was more than a duplicate of himself down to the last spot, Philippe thought. Louis was his brother—his kinsman. And Philippe was about to take part in that brother's kidnapping.

Philippe felt horrible. This wasn't the way someone ought to treat his brother, he thought. It wasn't the way one ought to treat *anyone.*

Worse, if all went according to Aramis's plan, Louis would be placed in prison, just as Philippe had been. And, just like Philippe, he would be forced to wear an iron mask all the rest of his days—by the order of the king himself.

And if Louis insisted that *he* was the king, no one would listen to him. After all, who would take the word of a lowly prisoner?

Philippe felt sorry for Louis, despite the cruelty the king had shown toward others. Philippe couldn't help it.

After all, he knew what it felt like to wear a heavy, uncomfortable mask and spend endless amounts of time in a dreary prison cell.

Unfortunately, the future of all France was at stake. Louis couldn't be allowed to remain king. He also couldn't be allowed to run free—and Philippe wouldn't stand for the idea of anyone killing his brother. The only other choice was to place Louis in the Bastille.

Just then, Louis stirred, no doubt disturbed by
some sound or smell in the room. As the king sat up in
his bed and blinked away sleep, he happened to look
in Philippe's direction. The sight of a masked man
made Louis's eyes open wide.

"Heavens!" he cried. "Who *are* you? What are you
doing in my—"

He never voiced the rest of his remark. Porthos
crossed the chamber in one big bound and pressed his
handkerchief against Louis's snout. The king struggled,
trying to claw the piece of cloth away with his paws,
but he didn't struggle for long. After a moment or two,
he slumped unconscious in the big man's strong arms.

"Quick!" Aramis rasped. "Remove his bedclothes.
I'll see to Philippe."

Porthos did as he was told, stripping off the king's
nightshirt and wig. At the same time, Aramis helped

Philippe slip out of his clothes. Last, they took off his mask.

Then, as quickly as they could, they put Philippe's clothes on his brother, and Louis's clothes and wig on Philippe. When at last they pulled the mask over Louis's head, the exchange was complete.

"There," Porthos whispered to Philippe. "Now you look more like the king than the king does—and the king looks more like you. That is to say, you both look like each other, but you look more like him than he looks like you."

Philippe wished the big man hadn't opened his mouth. "I'm so confused," he said.

"Don't say that," Aramis warned him. "You can't afford to be confused. You must play your role now, and play it well, or all our heads will roll."

Philippe pulled himself together. "You can count on me," he said.

Suddenly, there was a knock at the bedroom door. "Your Majesty?" came a muffled voice from the other side.

Philippe looked at his friends. They looked back at him—and Aramis mouthed a single, silent word: *D'Artagnan!*

In a second, Porthos had swept Louis up in his arms and slipped through the open panel in the wall. Aramis was right on his heels—though he paused long enough to watch Philippe leap into bed and pull the covers up with his teeth.

"Good luck," he whispered. Then he closed the panel behind him.

A second time, someone knocked on the door. Philippe took a deep breath, sat up in bed, and said, "Come in."

115

The door swung open and a man in dark clothes appeared on the threshold. He had wavy hair and piercing dark eyes. It was D'Artagnan, all right, just as Philippe had pictured him—and he had a sword dangling from his belt.

The captain of the guards looked around the Chamber of Morpheus. Then he turned to Philippe.

"Your Majesty," he explained, "I heard sounds in your bedchamber. I was compelled to investigate."

Philippe could feel D'Artagnan's gaze scouring him with its dark intensity. Picking him apart. Analyzing him like an exotic insect. For a long, terrible moment, he felt certain the captain of the guards had recognized him as an impostor.

In fact, Philippe thought, sinking farther into his bedcovers, *he's probably figured out the whole scheme. In a second or two, he'll search the room, find the secret panel, and send his men after Aramis and Porthos. And not long after, the three of us will be hanging from a gallows.*

Then King Louis would be rescued from the prison at the Bastille. He would be sitting on his throne again tomorrow as he had earlier that day, stepping on people's rights and throwing his weight around. Making a mockery of France. . . .

I can't let that happen, Philippe decided. *I can't lie around and wait for D'Artagnan to find something suspicious about me.*

Philippe kicked back the bedcovers and sat up straight in bed. "As you can see," he said, mimicking his brother's arrogant tone of voice, "there's no one in here but me. If it's all right with you, D'Artagnan, I'd like to get some sleep."

The captain of the guards gazed at him a moment longer. Then he bowed his head. "As you wish, Your Majesty." And he backed out of the room, closing the door behind him.

Yesss! thought Philippe. *I did it! I faked him out of his boots!*

Then the door opened again—and D'Artagnan let himself back into the room. "Just one other matter, my king."

Philippe composed himself. "And that is . . . ?" he demanded.

"My old friend Aramis asked me if he could see you first thing tomorrow morning. I explained to him that I was not the person in charge of your schedule. Still, Aramis is a clever man, and he often has good ideas."

Philippe paused for a moment. Then he nodded.

"I'll see him," he told D'Artagnan. "That is, if your friend is as clever as you say he is."

D'Artagnan bowed again. "Thank you, Your Majesty. And good night."

The captain of the guards left the elegant chamber again and closed the door after him. This time, it was for good.

Philippe breathed a sigh of relief. Settling back into bed, he began to get used to the idea that he was the king of France.

Of course, he still felt for his brother Louis, despite the fellow's wicked ways. However, Louis's fate would be no worse than the one Philippe had suffered at his brother's hands.

Besides, Philippe told himself, *I have more important things to think about. The future of my country is at stake.* He spent the rest of the night dreaming about what he would do in the morning.

When the sun rose, so did Philippe. In fact, he got up so early that he surprised his valets. Apparently, Louis was used to sleeping late.

Philippe made a mental note to remember that item. He didn't want to do anything that would arouse anyone's suspicions.

As the valets helped Philippe get dressed, he went over the list Aramis had given him—but only in his mind, of course. Then he took a deep breath and entered the throne room, the chamber where he would receive his visitors. He approached the king's chair slowly, struggling to hide his nervousness and excitement. Finally, he leaped onto it and waited.

His mother entered the room first. She was followed by his younger brother—the Duc d'Orléans—and his sister-in-law, Henrietta. Philippe had been expecting all of them.

However, he was unprepared for the emotions that the sight of his mother aroused in him. The day before, he had seen her only from afar. Now she was up close, looking into his face as if she feared what he would do to her.

Philippe resolved to treat his mother better than his brother Louis had. Approaching her, he lifted his paw. When his mother reached to shake it, he gave her hand a gentle lick.

"I hope my mother slept well," he said. "After all, nothing in the world is more important to me than your happiness."

The queen mother looked at Philippe with surprise—

but it was a pleasant kind of surprise. "You know," she said, "you sound much like your father today."

"I take that as a compliment," he told her. Then he turned to his younger brother and Henrietta and addressed them both with affection and respect.

They, too, looked at him with some surprise. But they didn't seem so shocked that they might have suspected anything.

A servant entered the chamber. "Your Majesty," he said, "the former musketeer known as Aramis is asking to see you."

The queen mother blushed. "I know this fellow," she told the king. "He is one of the three brave men who performed such wonders alongside our own D'Artagnan."

"Yes," said Philippe, "he is." Very soon, Aramis would be his prime minister, though it wasn't the time or place to announce that. "See him in," Philippe told the servant.

The man bowed and left. A moment later, he came back with Aramis. The man with the beard knelt in the king's presence.

"I'm honored that you would consent to see me, Your Majesty," said Aramis.

"Well," said Philippe, "I've heard you're a clever man. At least, that's what my officer D'Artagnan tells me, and I respect his opinion."

It felt funny to be speaking with his friend this way. But from that moment on, it was an act they would have to keep up, at least in front of others.

Aramis smiled. "You are too kind, my lord." He got to his feet. "Now, if Your Majesty has some time, I have a number of ideas that may improve France's situation with regard to the rest of Europe."

The king smiled back at him. "My dear Aramis, I have nothing *but* time."

Inside, Philippe was happier than he had been in a very long time. No one seemed to suspect that he was not Louis. His family and his servants all believed he was the king. Even D'Artagnan believed it. He had to concentrate to keep his tail from wagging uncontrollably.

But he knew it would not be enough merely to sit on the throne. He wanted to become the smartest, kindest, most helpful king he could be.

So great a task, he knew, would take some work— in fact, a lifetime's worth. . . .

Chapter Thirteen

Wishbone was still dreaming about Philippe when he woke up on Tuesday morning. He noticed that Joe hadn't slept with his catcher's mask the night before. Also, he seemed especially eager to get ready for school.

Ellen seemed to notice the change, too. "What's your rush?" she asked Joe.

Joe looked up at her from his bowl of corn flakes. "I need to speak to Mr. Kuperstein before class."

His mother looked at him. "The teacher?"

Joe nodded. "About the debate. I need to tell him I still want to do it."

"Debate?" Ellen said helplessly.

"Uh-huh," Joe managed to answer between gulps of cereal. "In front of the whole sixth grade. To see who'll make the best class president."

His mom smiled. "You're running for class president? Why haven't I heard anything about this before?"

Joe looked at Wishbone. The boy seemed grateful

for what his friend had done. "I guess I just realized how important it was."

"'Atta boy!" said Wishbone.

Joe looked at his mom, his face scrunching up with curiosity. "Say, you were in the sixth grade once."

Ellen nodded. "A couple of hundred years ago."

The boy smiled. "Seriously, Mom. What was it like? Would you say sixth-graders in your time had it better or worse than we have it today?"

Ellen thought for a moment. "Tell you what, Joe. I'll give that question some thought. We can talk about it after school."

"Great," he said.

Then he kissed his mom, grabbed his backpack, and bolted out the door. Wishbone was hot on his pal's heels—and was he excited!

After all, he thought, *this is the first time I've ever been on the campaign trail.*

Wishbone couldn't go into school with Joe, but he waited outside like the faithful dog he was. When Joe came out of the door at three o'clock, the boy looked happy.

"He must have convinced Mr. Kuperstein to hold the debate," Wishbone guessed.

Joe picked up Wishbone and hugged him. Then he set him down.

"Guess what!" Joe said with obvious enthusiasm. "I convinced Mr. Kuperstein to hold the debate."

"I thought so," said Wishbone.

The Jack Russell terrier wagged his tail with joy. Joe was finally doing what he should have done in the beginning. He was giving that troublemaking Damont a run for his money.

"Hey!" a familiar voice called to them.

Wishbone turned and saw Damont. "What does *he* want?" the dog wondered.

Damont had an annoyed expression on his face as he walked up to Joe. "Tell me I didn't hear what I thought I heard," he said.

Joe shrugged. "What did you *think* you heard?"

"That you were still running against me," Damont replied. "But of course, that's ridiculous. Everybody knows you can't campaign for class president and practice with the traveling baseball team at the same time."

Joe nodded. "You're right. That's why I've decided not to go out for the traveling team."

Damont's eyes widened. "Not go out? But . . . haven't you wanted to play for that team all your life?"

"That's true," said Joe. "But sixth-graders can't play for the team this year. Coach Bernardi told me so himself."

Damont swallowed hard. "Oh."

"He also spoke with Red, Lefty, and Flip," Joe said. "It turns out they knew I couldn't play for the team. But someone paid them to make me *think* I could—so I wouldn't have time to run for class president." His eyes narrowed. "Now, who do you think would do a thing like that?"

Damont frowned. "Okay, so you caught me. I only did it because I wanted the best man to win. And I'm obviously the best man."

"We'll see about that," Joe told him.

"Yeah," Wishbone chimed in. "We'll see about that, indeed."

The next morning came more quickly than Wishbone had imagined it could.

"Time flies when your pal is running for class president," he observed. He watched Joe and David enter the school building.

Wishbone knew the debate would take place first thing that day. In minutes, the whole sixth grade would be gathering in the auditorium, eager to hear what Joe and Damont had to say for themselves.

Fortunately, it was still warm out, so the windows of the auditorium were open. Wishbone was able to leap up onto a window ledge and peek inside.

The auditorium was a big room with more seats than Wishbone had ever seen in his life. It had a big stage, too, with three standing microphones set up on it.

At first, all the seats were empty. Pretty soon, though, the sixth-graders began filing in and sitting down. Before long, the place was packed.

"And why not?" the terrier asked. "This has got to be the best show in town."

Moments later, he saw three people come out on the stage. Joe was one of them. The other two were Damont and Mr. Kuperstein, one of the sixth-grade teachers.

Mr. Kuperstein was a tall, thin man who wore thick glasses. He wasn't known for his sense of humor.

The teacher took up a position behind the microphone at the center of the stage. Each of the boys stopped at one of the other microphones.

"Here we go," said Wishbone, his tail wagging with excitement.

Tapping his microphone to make sure it was working, Mr. Kuperstein smoothed the front of his sport jacket and addressed the sixth-grade class.

"As you know," he said, "your classmates Damont Jones and Joe Talbot are competing for the office of class president. The purpose of this brief debate is to give the two of them a chance to speak to you—to let you know where they stand on the issues."

From Wishbone's point of view, Damont looked pretty confident. It had to have come as a surprise to Damont that Joe would go ahead with the debate. But if he was nervous, the Damonster didn't show it.

Joe, on the other hand, kept tugging at his collar, as if it were too tight. Wishbone's pal looked *plenty* nervous.

"Stay cool, Joe," said the terrier. "You're the better candidate. You've just got to show it."

"First," Mr. Kuperstein said, "we'll hear our candidates' opening statements." He glanced at Damont. "Mr. Jones?"

Before Damont could even get started, the kids in the audience began to clap for him as loud as they could. A couple even cheered for Damont. It took a while for Mr. Kuperstein to stare the audience into silence.

"Let's have no more outbursts," he told them, "or we will skip this debate altogether."

"Wow!" said Wishbone, surprised by the number of voters Damont had attracted. "You give out a few ice-cream certificates, and you've got yourself a following. But as someone once said, you can't fool all of the people all of the time."

He was confident that Joe would win over the voters. It would just take some work.

"As sixth-graders," said Damont, making his opening statement into the microphone, "we need to work together to make our school a better place. We need to make our community a better place, too."

Mr. Kuperstein turned to Joe. "Mr. Talbot?"

Joe cleared his throat. His microphone screeched with feedback, a sure sign that his mouth was too close to it.

"I . . . er . . . agree with Damont," he told the audience. "We need to do the things he said."

As Joe paused, Wishbone heard the assembled sixth-graders shifting in their chairs. They were waiting for Joe to say something Damont hadn't already said before him.

"Is that your entire opening statement?" asked Mr. Kuperstein.

Joe nodded. "That's it."

"I see," said the teacher. He turned to Damont again. "Now, Mr. Jones, how do you propose to achieve these worthwhile objectives?"

Damont smiled even more confidently than before. "I'm glad you asked that question, sir. You see, I have a vision for our sixth grade here in Oakdale. Under my leadership, our sixth-grade class will go down in history as the best sixth grade this school has ever known."

Mr. Kuperstein harrumphed. "Can you be a little more specific, Mr. Jones?"

Damont's smile faded a bit. "Specific, sir? Uh . . . in what way?"

"Specific," said the teacher, "in terms of how you're going to make all this happen. What are you going to do—on a day-to-day basis, I mean?"

"On a day-to-day basis," Damont replied, "I'm

going to make people proud of us." He lifted his chin as he addressed the audience. "I'm going to make our teachers proud of us. I'm going to make our parents proud of us. And I'm going to make us proud of ourselves."

Mr. Kuperstein looked at Damont for a moment, a sour expression on his face. Then he turned to Joe.

"And you, Mr. Talbot? How are you going to benefit your school and your community?"

Joe took a deep breath. "Well," he said, "I think everything Damont has mentioned is worthwhile."

Again, Wishbone heard the kids shifting in their seats. They were getting impatient, and the terrier didn't blame them.

Mr. Kuperstein sighed. "Don't you have any thoughts of your own, Mr. Talbot?"

Joe nodded. "Yessir, I do. I was just getting to them." He swallowed. "You see, I did some research—mainly by talking to my mom—and I found out sixth-graders used to be able to do a lot of things they can't do anymore."

That got Mr. Kuperstein's attention. "Is that so? Can you give me an example?"

"Yessir," said Joe. "As you know, sixth-graders can't work on the school newspaper. They could work on it a long time ago, but some of those sixth-graders let their grades slip. So the principal said they couldn't work for the paper anymore."

The teacher's eyes narrowed. "And you want to change that?"

Joe nodded again. "I think today's sixth-graders are responsible enough to work on the paper *and* keep their grades up. All we need is a chance to prove it."

There was a spattering of applause throughout the

audience. At a glance from Mr. Kuperstein, everyone quieted down again.

"And that's not all," Joe said. "Until eight or nine years ago, the sixth-graders used to have a band concert. We don't have that anymore."

"That's true," said the teacher. "It's because we can't afford it. There's just not enough money in the budget."

"That's right," Damont chimed in. "A band concert would be great, but money doesn't grow on trees."

"We can *raise* the money," Joe insisted, "by having a sixth-grade candy drive. Then we don't need to take any money out of the budget."

Mr. Kuperstein was starting to look impressed. This time, when some of the kids in the audience started applauding, he wasn't quite so quick to make them stop.

"That's very interesting," the teacher told Joe.

"Thank you, sir," said Joe. "But I'm not done yet." He turned to the audience again. "Holding a band concert and working on the newspaper will make things better for us and for our school. But we've also got an obligation to Oakdale.

"A while back, every grade used to put together a project for Earth Day. That stopped, for some reason. I'd like to get it going again, and I think the sixth grade is where it should start. All we have to do is get together and clean up a place in town that needs some help. It shouldn't take more than a few hours, if we all pitch in."

"Right," Damont muttered under his breath. "Like kids are really going to do all that work for nothing."

Joe looked at him. "It's not for nothing, Damont. It's so we can make our town a better place to live. Or have you changed your mind about that?"

As Damont scowled at him, Joe looked at the audience. "What do you think? Are you willing to put in the work? Are you willing to lead the way for all the other grades?"

For a moment, there was silence. Then, way in the back, a couple of kids started clapping. Wishbone saw it was David and Samantha.

A few more kids began applauding, and then a few more. Before Wishbone knew it, the entire auditorium was thundering with the sound of clapping hands.

Even Mr. Kuperstein had to smile. He looked at the two candidates. "Well," he said, "thank you for your comments, gentlemen. You've certainly given us food for thought."

"That's for sure," Wishbone said from his perch on the window ledge. "Now, how about some food for *eating*. All this debating is really making me hungry."

Chapter Fourteen

The election for sixth-grade class president took place at lunchtime on Thursday, a day after the debate.

Wishbone had been pacing in front of the school all day long, his tail wagging furiously. David and Samantha had joined him when school let out.

But not Joe. He and Damont had been asked to meet with the principal in his office. It was a tradition that the principal told the candidates the election results before they were announced to everyone else.

Wishbone knew Joe had done a good job in the debate the day before, but he was still far from being a shoe-in. Joe didn't have any of the gimmicks Damont had. All he could do was tell his classmates how hard he was willing to work for them.

"What do you think?" asked Samantha, shading her eyes to stare in the direction of the school's front door.

David kicked at a rock and shrugged. "I don't know. Joe *did* get into the race kind of late. And Damont had all those really cool posters and bumper stickers and stuff."

Sam sighed. "Don't forget the free ice-cream certificates."

David nodded. "Those, too."

The two of them looked worried. Wishbone had to admit he was a little concerned himself.

He remembered what he'd learned from *The Man in the Iron Mask*—that the good guys can come out on top when they do what's needed of them. In the end, at least, Joe had tried his best to do what was needed of him.

But had he done it in time? That was the question.

Wait a second, Wishbone thought, perking up suddenly. *What am I thinking? Joe's the candidate with the mostest. He's the kid with all the good ideas. He's gonna win hands down, no question about it.*

Suddenly, he saw Joe's face appear in the little glass window in the school's front door. The boy opened the door and emerged into the bright sunshine.

Wishbone knew Joe as well as anybody. He searched his buddy's face for a sign of which way the election had gone. But try as he might, he couldn't find any. Joe just seemed . . . well, stunned.

Wishbone couldn't wait for the boy to walk up to him. He bolted up the walk and leaped into Joe's arms. Surprised, Joe stumbled a bit, but he managed to catch Wishbone anyway.

"So what happened?" the terrier said excitedly. "Come on, already! Don't keep us in suspense!"

Samantha and David were a few steps behind Wishbone. They wanted to know what was going on, as well. David had his fingers crossed for good luck. Sam's face was one big question.

"Well?" she asked.

"Yeah," said David, "what's the verdict?"

Joe didn't answer right away. He seemed to be in shock. Finally, he put some words together.

"I won," he told his friends.

"You *won?*" David whooped, his eyes nearly popping out of his head. "You *really* won?"

Joe smiled a little, as the significance of what had happened started to sink in. "Uh-huh. That's what the principal told me. It was really close—the closest election in years. But I won."

Just then, the news was repeated over the school's public address system. Everyone inside and outside the building heard the results of the election.

"Joe Talbot is our new sixth-grade class president," said the principal. "I hope his classmates will give him all their support. I also want to congratulate Damont Jones, the runner-up. . . ."

"This calls for a celebration," Wishbone said. "Water and dog biscuits for everyone!"

Then Damont came outside. He didn't look happy at all as he walked over to Joe.

At first, Wishbone thought Damont would say Joe cheated. After all, that was the Damonster's style.

"He'll probably demand a recount," Wishbone said.

As it turned out, Damont didn't ask for anything of the sort. He took Joe's hand and shook it.

"Congratulations," Damont said.

Joe studied him for a moment. Then he replied, "Thanks."

Damont frowned. "I guess you're still pretty mad at me for that stunt I pulled. I can't say I blame you."

Joe shrugged. "You made a mistake. Nobody's perfect."

"'Atta boy," said Wishbone. "You're the winner, Joe. You may as well be a gracious one."

David, on the other hand, wasn't quite so willing to forgive. "If I were you," he told Damont, "I'd clean up my act."

At that moment, someone nearby cleared his throat. Wishbone turned to locate the origin of the sound. It took less than a second for him to realize it had come from Officer Krulla.

The policeman beckoned to Damont with his forefinger. He had a "Damont Delivers" campaign poster rolled up in his other hand.

"Let's go," said Officer Krulla. "You've got a lot of

work ahead of you, Damont. There are posters like this one all over the place."

Wishbone leaped up on his hind legs. "I guess it's not just Damont's act he's going to have to clean up. It's the whole town!"

He watched as Damont and Officer Krulla headed for the nearest campaign poster.

About Alexandre Dumas

From an early age, Alexandre Dumas was fascinated with two kinds of stories—the tales of adventure and courage that ran in his family, and the histories of the kings and queens who ruled France hundreds of years earlier. It was only natural that he would combine the two when he became a professional story-teller years later.

Born in July 1802, Dumas was the product of two generations of adventurous men. His grandfather, the Marquis de la Pailleterie, left France for the Caribbean in the eighteenth century to seek new fortune. The marquis's son, Alexandre-Thomas, a tall, muscular, fearless fellow, won renown as a high-ranking military officer under Napoleon Bonaparte.

The same love of adventure led Dumas, a big, handsome man with curly black hair, to move from his country home to Paris. There, he began writing plays on historical topics at the age of twenty-one. The public loved his work and flocked to see his productions.

By the time Dumas turned to writing historical novels in the 1840s, he had developed a talent for glamorizing history—in other words, making it seem more bright and exciting than it actually was.

From 1842 to 1852, Dumas wrote some of the world's best-loved adventure novels, including *The Count of Monte Christo* and *The Black Tulip* (1850). However, he's best known for *The Three Musketeers* and its sequels—*Twenty Years After* and *The Man in the Iron Mask*.

Dumas was an outspoken supporter of democratic causes in France. He sided with the revolutions that took place in 1830 and 1870. *The Man in the Iron Mask* was written during the second of those events, partly to protest the way the French leaders were abusing their power.

After suffering a stroke in the spring of 1870, Dumas died at the home of his son on December 5 of the same year. He is remembered as a man who had a talent for telling stories and a deep appreciation of life's romantic possibilities.

About *The Man in the Iron Mask*

In the 1840s, there was a folktale about a man forced to wear a mask so no one could see what he looked like. According to the story, which some historians believe might have some truth to it, this man was later jailed in the Paris prison known as the Bastille—though no one could say why.

This was just the sort of romantic mystery that tickled Alexandre Dumas's fancy. Before long, he had combined the legend of the man in the mask with the historical actions of France's King Louis XIV and the exploits of his favorite characters, the so-called Three Musketeers.

One might ask how Dumas could know what it was like to languish in the Bastille with an iron mask on his face. After all, he himself had never been thrown in jail.

However, his father—a tall, muscular officer in the army of Napoleon Bonaparte—spent two years in an Italian prison. When the elder Dumas finally came home, he was a broken man, having lost his health and his immense strength. His ordeal left a lasting impression on young Alexandre.

The Man in the Iron Mask was first published as a series of newspaper installments, beginning in 1848 and ending in 1850. At the time, it was called *Le Vicomte de Bragelonne.*

Actually, the story of Philippe, the prince who was forced to suffer in prison while his twin brother sat on the throne, was only part of the tale. *The Man in the Iron Mask* also told of the final adventures of the musketeers Athos, Porthos, Aramis, and D'Artagnan, who had been the main characters in two of the author's earlier novels.

As with many of his works, Dumas also had some help producing *The Man in the Iron Mask*. Auguste Maquet, a former history teacher, is credited with doing much of the research and writing that went into the novel. It was Dumas, however, who gave the story its most adventurous touches.

It comes as no surprise that Wishbone would feel a kinship with the long-suffering Philippe. Despite everything he went through, Philippe always kept his chin up. And when the chips were down, he was willing to risk everything for the sake of his friends.

The Man in the Iron Mask is an exciting story of mystery, honor, and adventure. It is peopled with unforgettable characters and set in one of the most interesting periods of French history. However, the tale has been read and reread by generations because we are touched by the plight of young Philippe.

All of us can only hope that, when the need arises, we will show ourselves to be as noble as the man in the iron mask.

About Michael Jan Friedman

Michael Jan Friedman, a *New York Times* best-selling author, has written or collaborated on thirty science fiction, fantasy, and young-adult novels over the course of his career. More than four million of his books are currently in print in the United States alone.

Friedman found writing *The Mutt in the Iron Muzzle* a special thrill. After all, Alexandre Dumas has always been one of his favorite writers, and *The Man in the Iron Mask* one of his favorite novels.

When he was a child, Friedman often fantasized about what it would be like to secretly be the heir to a great throne. By reading *The Man in the Iron Mask,* he was able to see that it might not be such a good thing, after all.

By the same token, Friedman has always been a fan of the humble and courageous Philippe, who risked everything—including his life—to remove his cruel and tyrannical twin brother from the throne.

Friedman became a freelance writer in 1985, after the publication of his first book, a heroic fantasy called *The Hammer and The Horn.* Since then, he has written for television, radio, magazines, and comic books, though his first love is still the novel.

A native New Yorker, Friedman received his undergraduate degree from the University of Pennsylvania, and his graduate degree from Syracuse University's Newhouse School. He lives with his wife and children on Long Island, where he spends his free time sailing on the Long Island Sound, jogging, and following his favorite baseball team, the New York Yankees.